Shirlee Smith Matheson

Shirlee Smith Matheson lived in northern British Columbia not far from the Alaska Highway, and has travelled the Highway from Mile Zero to Fairbanks. She has written and published numerous short stories for young people and adults, several plays, as well as award-winning nonfiction books for adults and a previous juvenile fiction book, *Prairie Pictures*.

Ms. Matheson currently lives in Calgary, Alberta.

Also by Shirlee Smith Matheson

Juvenile Fiction
Prairie Pictures

Adult Nonfiction
Youngblood of the Peace
This Was Our Valley

Shirlee Smith Matheson

Flying GHOSTS

Shirlee Smith Matheson

Stoddart

Published in 1993 by Stoddart Publishing Co. Limited

Published in Canada in 2001 by
Stoddart Kids, a division of
Stoddart Publishing Co. Limited
895 Don Mills Road, 400-2 Park Centre, Toronto, Ontario M3C 1W3

Published in the United States in 2001 by
Stoddart Kids, a division of
Stoddart Publishing Co. Limited
PMB 128, 4500 Witmer Estates, Niagara Falls, New York 14305-1386

www.stoddartkids.com

To order Stoddart books please contact General Distribution Services
In Canada Tel. (416) 213-1919 Fax (416) 213-1917
Email cservice@genpub.com
In the United States Toll-free tel. 1-800-805-1083
Toll-free fax 1-800-481-6207
Email gdsinc@genpub.com

05 04 03 02 01   2 3 4 5

Canadian Cataloguing in Publication Data

Matheson, Shirlee Smith
Flying ghosts

ISBN 0-7736-7400-4

I. Title

PS8576.A82F59 1993   jC813'.54   C93-094467-4
PR9199.3.M37F59 1993

Cover design: Brant Cowie/ArtPlus Limited
Cover illustration: Stephen Quick

The characters in this book are fictitious, with the exception
of a few famous bush pilots and U.S. Army personnel.

Headlines and excerpts at the beginning of chapters originally
appeared in the Calgary *Herald* from December 1941 to October 1942,
except for the excerpt on page 47, which appeared
in the San Francisco *Chronicle*.

We acknowledge for their financial support of our publishing program
the Government of Canada through the Book Publishing
Industry Development Program (BPIDP), the Canada Council,
and the Ontario Arts Council.

Printed and bound in Canada by Webcom Ltd.

To Ruth Andrishak and Elona Malterre,
my Banff buddies who fly with me in uncharted skies

In tribute to northern bush pilots . . .

The nameless men who nameless rivers travel,
And in strange valleys greet strange deaths alone;
The grim, intrepid ones who would unravel
The mysteries that shroud the polar zone.

— Robert Service,
"To the Man of the High North"

Contents

Acknowledgements

Most goals need an assist. The following people helped me make this story as authentic as if it really happened . . .

The late Earl K. Pollon, Hudson's Hope, B.C., for sharing scenes of traplines and traders, operatic dogs and screaming sawmills, shrews, mink and marten, and other creatures of the North.

Gerri Young of Fort Nelson, B.C., for her book *The Fort Nelson Story* and for checking over scenes relevant to the area.

Pilots Thomas Legg of Calgary, Alberta; Pen Powell of Hudson's Hope, B.C.; Wally Wolfe of Yellowknife, N.W.T. And especially Jimmy "Midnight" Anderson of Mile 147, Alaska Highway (Pink Mountain, B.C.), whose nickname and sayings have been used, with his permission, to bring to life the character of Matthew "Midnight" Smith. Jimmy also checked over every detail of the book as carefully as he checked over his Super-Cub before he flew it in the exact same areas as Midnight Smith flies his Norseman . . . including the mysterious Valley.

Special thanks to Ruth Andrishak, Komarno, Manitoba, for her faith in the manuscript and in my ability to tell this story.

THE ALASKA HIGHWAY

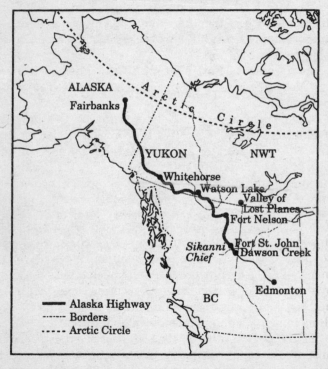

1

The Wolf Man

CASUALTIES BRING WAR HOME TO U.S.

The United States — united at last under savage
and treacherous attack — closed ranks behind
its president to fight to the finish a "total war"
with Japan, with Britain, Canada and Pacific
dominions full allies in the Pacific War.

Winter in Alaska is a time of secrets, when sounds become
important because there are so few. In the thin, clean air
sounds carry for miles — trees snapping, dogs howling,
men calling, shotguns blasting, and bush planes buzzing
over white valleys. But when the storms come, you hear
nothing but the wind screaming in fury as it lashes everything in its path and piles snow in high drifts.

That day, December 8, 1941, the north wind shrieked
around our cabin, whipping blasts of snow against the
windows. Above the din we heard a crash and the sound
of wood splintering.

I jumped up. "What's that?"

"Sounds like the wind's ripping the roof off the shed!"
Dad rushed to the peg for his coat, then stopped. "What's

the use." He spun a kitchen chair around and, straddling it, thumped down, facing its back.

The pack dogs started howling, their chains clanking against the trees they were tethered to.

"What's got into those fool animals?" Mom asked.

Then, over the dogs' howls we could hear the staccato sound of an engine. I opened the door carefully, but the wind grabbed it from me and smashed it against the cabin wall. Mom scooped up Jody and took her into the bedroom, away from the draft.

The drone, low over our cabin now, became deafening. The sound seemed to fade a bit, then grew louder again toward the end of the lake.

"Some fool's trying to get himself killed!" Dad grabbed his mackinaw and ran outside, down onto the ice, waving his arms. I followed.

Through the swirling snow I could just make out the shape of an airplane. The flying ghost dipped its wings toward us, then turned and roared over our heads, brushing the treetops beyond the cabin. Again the airplane approached the lake, the wind slewing its broad wings as the pilot wrestled to bring it down.

I could make out its call letters now: NC-195N, black against the yellow tail. The skis hit the frozen lake, and the airplane bounced twice before it finally glued itself to the snow and skidded to a stop before us. The propeller slowed, then stopped, but no one emerged from the big yellow airplane shuddering on our frozen beach. Dad and I ran down and held on to the wing struts so it wouldn't fly off again or flip over.

At last the door flew open. Someone wearing a black wolf-fur parka ducked through the doorway, then dropped to the ground.

"Who on earth is this?" Dad said.

The Wolf Man stripped off his beaded moosehide mitt

and extended his right hand in greeting. Neither Dad nor I moved.

"Aren't you going to shake your brother's hand?" the pilot said.

Dad stood staring for a moment, then went up to the man and peered through the fur, trying to get a look at the half-hidden face. "So it took you twenty years to find me." He clasped the outstretched hand.

"I was just out for a Sunday cruise in my Norseman when I saw your camp." The Wolf Man laughed and turned to me. "You must be Jed's boy."

"Yes. I'm Jay."

"Well, I'm your Uncle Matthew. And I've come for a long overdue visit."

Uncle? I had an uncle? Before I knew what was happening, I was smothered in cold fur that smelled of gasoline and fish. My uncle released me with a slap on the shoulder. "Ah, you look just like your dad before he left home!" He turned to Dad. "Glad to see me?"

Dad looked away. When he answered, his reply was almost cut off by the wind. "You're here now. Yeah. I'm glad . . ."

"Then let's put this baby to bed and get inside where it's warm!"

My uncle climbed back inside the airplane and threw out some ropes and a canvas cover for the engine. We helped him secure the plane to the wharf so it wouldn't flip over in the wind. He tossed his duffel bag and bedroll toward me. "Take these in, please, Jay. I have to drain the oil."

I picked up the bag and bedroll and walked up the hill to our cabin. It would look pretty shabby to a stranger: a two-room log shack with a pitched roof, cross-cut saw and traps hanging from the outside wall, dog toboggan and snowshoes up against the side. Our food and pelt cache stood high on stilts, overlooking the cabin and shed where we kept the dogs' harnesses and food, old traps, and stuff.

The dogs were quiet now, sensing that the metal monster and its master were here to stay. I pulled open the heavy wooden door and entered the cabin, throwing the gear onto the floor.

"Mom, it's Dad's brother!"

Mom turned away from the window where she had been watching. "Your dad knew this would happen someday." Her voice sounded kind of strange.

Dad and my uncle came in carrying a pail of engine oil drained from the airplane. "It's got to be kept warm, just like us," my uncle said. Then, seeing Mom, he smiled.

Mom extended her hand. "I'm Lilly. This is Joanna, but we call her Jody."

"I'm Matthew. Pleased to meet you, sister-in-law!" He reached out, encircling her and my little sister in a big bear hug. They almost disappeared in the black fur of his parka.

I turned and looked at Dad standing in the doorway, his outline framed by flying snow. He seemed kind of scared, and angry, way different from how I'd be if a long-lost brother had found me!

But maybe he knew the arrival of the Wolf Man at our trapline cabin in eastern Alaska would change our lives forever.

2

War Declared

We were sitting around the table, talking, getting to know each other. Uncle Matthew told me I looked a lot like Dad when he was my age. I was five foot eight, and my shoulders had widened in the last year. All three of us had dark hair and light blue eyes, but he and Dad had crow's-feet that crinkled when they smiled. Uncle Matthew had a straight nose — it hadn't been broken like Dad's — high cheekbones, and nice white teeth, like me.

As we talked, Dad was repairing a dog harness, Mom was making supper, and I just sat listening, fascinated. Normally I'd be doing homework. I was taking ninth grade by correspondence, with Mom tutoring, but I sure wouldn't be able to concentrate with my uncle here. Until today, I hadn't even known Dad had a brother. Maybe I had cousins, too.

"Are you married, Uncle Matt?" I asked.

"Just to that lady out there, Jay." He nodded toward the Norseman. "She's my only girl. I give her all my time, all my money, and tell her all my dreams." He laughed.

"How long have you been flying?"

"About fifteen years."

"Gee, as long as I've been alive. How did you get to be a pilot?"

"Don't get any ideas," Mom said.

"I took my flight training at the Washington Flying School out of Seattle. Father was furious." He looked over at Dad. "When you didn't come back, he expected me to take over the lumber operation."

"So we both got what we wanted," Dad said, "and the old man got what he deserved."

"Every time I see him, he asks if I've found you."

"I didn't want to be found then, and I'm not so sure I do yet."

Uncle Matthew leaned forward in his chair. "You could have been dead for all we knew. If only you'd written Mom."

"I tried," Dad said. "The letters came back marked 'delivery refused' in the old man's handwriting. I even sent messages with guys going to Seattle to let Mom know I was okay. Then one of the miners returned and told me she'd died. With her gone, nobody in the world seemed to care about me."

"You're wrong," Uncle Matthew said, and the room grew quiet. Jody stopped banging her high chair; Mom paused, the paring knife held still. Even the storm seemed to hold its breath. Dad sat looking down at his rough hands holding the harness.

"I flew all over Alaska asking people if they knew you."

"All seventy thousand of them?"

Uncle Matthew looked at Dad. I felt embarrassed by the sarcasm in my father's voice.

"I'm always flying miners and equipment in and out of the North — Yukon and Porcupine rivers, camps at Howling Dog, Old Rampart, Burnt Paw," Uncle Matthew said. "I heard a Jedediah Smith had a claim near Eagle, but it seemed you'd disappeared."

"Yes, Jed and I lived there," Mom said, ignoring Dad's warning look, ". . . for a while."

Uncle Matthew looked from one to the other. "I took supplies in to Mackenzie's trading post this morning, and Eureka! In the mail I brought was your catalogue order! They told me you were trapping just thirty miles down the Tanana River. After all this time no little snowstorm was going to stop me."

"Well, I'm glad you made it through the storm," Dad said, "but I — we — kind of keep to ourselves here."

Uncle Matthew jumped out of his chair, reached over, and ruffled Dad's hair. I was shocked. A look of irritation came over Dad's face, then he smiled. Jody threw her blocks into the air, and I tried hard to hide a grin.

"Your dad's a great guy," Uncle Matthew said to me. "Our old man was a slave-driver, but I can recall Jed sticking up for me. Then, he left."

"You can stay here with us now. Teach me to fly!" I said.

Uncle Matthew got serious. "You don't have a radio, do you?"

"No."

"Yesterday morning the Japanese attacked Pearl Harbour. Three hundred sixty planes bombed the smithereens out of the place. We're in the war, Jed. You, me, every American on the planet. And we've got to fight."

Dad looked up. "Pearl Harbour?"

"Hawaii. That's home turf."

"Good God. But . . . I got no more fight in me, Matt. And I'm too old to be of service."

Uncle Matthew took a copy of the Los Angeles *Times* from his duffle bag. The headlines were two inches high.

IT'S WAR!
HOSTILITIES DECLARED BY JAPANESE,
350 REPORTED KILLED IN HONOLULU RAID
AIR BOMBS RAINED ON PACIFIC BASES

Dad frowned. "So America's in it now!"

"That means we all have to pitch in . . . you, me, Lilly, even Jay," Uncle Matthew said.

"Doing what?" Dad threw the paper onto the table. The black headlines seemed to come alive under the light from the kerosene lamp.

"Building a highway. A military supply route from Dawson Creek, B.C., to Fairbanks, Alaska."

"When?"

"Right now!" Uncle Matthew stood up and raised his hands to grip the overhead log beam that ran from one side of the cabin to the other. It made him look seven feet tall. "I'm already flying personnel and supplies from one end of the country to the other. We've established the Northwest Staging Route, airports from Edmonton, Alberta, through to Alaska. The highway deal — a joint project between the States and Canada — is being negotiated right now. Japanese aircraft have been sighted in the San Francisco Bay area and up in the Aleutian Islands. If they think they'll find us with our pants down when they come swooping in from the Aleutians, they've got another think coming. This is the North! We don't sit around with our — " he looked around at Mom and me, " — our fingers in our ears."

"What can I do?" Dad sounded as if he was waiting for a secret assignment.

"You can help provide timber for this highway," Uncle Matthew said. "It's going to be a tough job building fifteen hundred miles of road through wilderness. I know I can get you on with a lumber camp. Think of the bridges and culverts needed — all made from wood. You got the know-how. Lilly could be the camp cook . . ." He smiled over at Mom. She didn't look pleased as she continued to fill coffee cups and set down supper. "Lilly could cook," Uncle Matthew insisted. "Even Jay could be bossing crews in a couple of weeks — "

"Jay's a boy," Mom said.

"Mom!"

"He looks stronger than a lot of men I've seen, and smarter." Uncle Matthew smiled at me. "How'd you like to earn a man's wage, Son, and still live at home?"

"Sure." Then I felt Mom's cold stare. "I can do my schoolwork at night."

Dad got up and started pacing. "I don't know, Matt. Sounds like it'll be a rough go. America in the war! Funny. We're living up here, closer to the Aleutians than anybody, and we didn't know a thing. Nothing here but miles of innocent country."

"Innocent country is right," Mom said. "What's this war got to do with us? We've got a good home here, and I'm not leaving it. And Jay isn't until he goes to high school in Fairbanks."

"It's going to be temporary work, Lilly." Dad was pleading now. "We could use the cash. You can't count on fur prices anymore."

"We've been managing. You rob Jay of an education and what will he be when the road's done? A jack of all trades, master of none! They're a dime a dozen in this country."

"It's our patriotic duty."

Mom picked Jody out of the high chair. "Bedtime, young lady," she said, and carried her into the bedroom. She slammed the door behind them.

"I'm sorry, Jed," Uncle Matthew said.

"That's all right. Maybe it's time for a little adventure." Dad's voice sounded defiant.

"That's a nice way of putting it. It'll be an adventure, all right. Just don't disappear on me again."

Uncle Matthew searched through his duffle bag and took out a rolled piece of oilcloth. He opened it to reveal a map of the world. "Here, Jay, this is for you. Put it up on the wall. You can stick pins in it to follow the fighting on all fronts."

"Thanks, Uncle Matt." Suddenly it felt like the outside world had jumped inside our cabin walls.

In bed that night I could hear Mom and Dad discussing the highway project, Mom protesting, Dad getting louder as he tried to convince her why we should leave the line.

"There's no money in trapping anymore, Lilly. You want Jay to get an education? All right! What's going to pay for it? Squirrel pelts? Might as well give away furs, market's like a yo-yo."

"But a sawmill . . . that's why you left home in the first place — "

"This is different. I can make some fast money, maybe buy in, be my own boss. And it's for the war! I'm an American."

"Well, Canada got in it two years ago, and you never thought about it too much then. I'm Canadian. Should I have enlisted?"

"Don't be silly." The house was silent except for the tick of the old clock, the crackle of wood in the stove, and the low moan of wind. "I'm going," Dad said.

That was the end of it.

All I really knew about my dad was that he'd left his home in Seattle at fifteen. My age. I wondered why. Maybe he'd felt the same call for adventure I did right now.

3

Learning Our Legends

The storm was still raging the next day. Uncle Matthew came outside at daybreak to help me feed the dogs. They were curled up in the snow, noses into tails, like fur doughnuts.

"Conda's our lead dog. She's the mother of the other three — Shiloh, Bess, and Brutus." I pointed them out as they jumped and yelped for attention.

"So Conda's special?" He reached over to pet her.

"She sure is. We've had her seven years, since she was a pup. She's Great Dane and wolf cross."

"Four dogs. What are you going to do with them when you leave?" He went over to Shiloh, who was lunging on his chain. The other two were in a frenzy of jealousy.

"Dad will still keep the trapline," I said defensively. "We're coming back."

Uncle Matthew stopped, as if considering the possibility. "I don't know if you will or not, Jay. This is a great place for a kid but not much for a young man. No friends around. Nothing to do."

I was about to tell him how Dad and I would trap

together in the winter, pan gold in the summer, pick berries, go fishing, cut and haul the winter's wood, and hunt in the fall. There were magazines and books. We knew what was going on. Still, we hadn't heard about America being in the war. Dad said we'd get a radio as soon as we could afford one. I looked around at our little camp, barely visible through the swirling snow. What if Uncle Matt was right?

"There's enough to do here," I replied finally. "I know the mountain trails, the rivers. I know about animals and birds. I can name the plants. I know everything I need to get along."

"Anything you don't know?" Uncle Matthew said with a grin. "Anything more you *might* want to learn?"

I shrugged. "Yeah. It would be neat to learn to fly . . . and maybe to build a highway."

"You can, Jay. And you can come back, too, if that's what you want."

The dogs were going crazy. I dropped the feed bucket and started playing with them. Four dogs weren't a large team, but they could haul a good load. And in winter they were our only transportation. We ran them strung out one behind the other, so they could pull the toboggan through narrow trails without getting tangled. Their harness was made of canvas because the dogs would eat leather.

"You good at running dogs?" Uncle Matthew asked.

"Pretty good. Conda's a great lead dog. We sometimes put Shiloh first and Conda second. Boy, does she educate him! He makes a wrong turn, she drags him the right way or he finds himself upside down!"

The dogs seemed to agree and barked like crazy. The cabin door flew open. Dad stomped over to us.

"What are you doing getting the dogs all riled up? You know better! They'll howl all day now."

"It was my fault. I started fooling with them," Uncle Matthew said.

"You're darn right it was. You may know airplanes, but you obviously don't know dogs!"

"Sorry, Jed — " he began, but I cut in.

"It wasn't his fault. I started playing with Brutus — " Dad's look stopped me.

"You two in some kind of conspiracy?" His eyes shot from me to Uncle Matthew. "Oh, I know. Hero comes in, stirs up everything, blasts off. You'll be howling for weeks. Just like these dogs. Well it's time you both got some sense of who calls the shots here!"

He turned and stomped back to the cabin. I couldn't look at Uncle Matthew.

"Hey, sorry Jay," he said softly. "I guess I forgot about his temper. And I did kind of crash in on you. After twenty years I had no right. I didn't think he'd be so resentful after all this time."

"It's okay. Dad — " but I couldn't say it. How do you say things like "Dad's jealous" to a stranger? Even if he is your uncle. "Dad's got to decide what trail to take."

Dad and Uncle Matthew had some private talks over the next couple of days and seemed to come to an understanding. But it was weird to have someone staying with us twenty-four hours a day in a two-room cabin. And even stranger that that someone was Dad's younger brother.

Sometimes I noticed Uncle Matthew looking at me from the corner of his eye, as if sizing me up, especially when he caught me looking at him, and then at myself in the mirror.

At first I felt shy around Uncle Matthew, not wanting to say something stupid, but it's hard to pretend you're smarter than you really are, day and night for three whole days. By the time the storm quit, I didn't care if he thought I was smart or not.

I asked him a hundred questions about flying. He showed me his pilot's logbook, where he recorded his licences and every flight. "This stays with me — always," he said. Then he showed me the aircraft log. "This is a record of every repair and check-up of the plane, and it stays with Nellie."

I flipped through them, reading the names of all the places he'd flown to — every part of Alaska, the Yukon, and Northwest Territories up to the Arctic coast, the western Canadian provinces to the prairies; down the B.C. coast into the northwestern states, and right across the States. My uncle had been everywhere, over prairies, oceans, and mountains.

"What happens if you crash in the mountains with no food," I asked, "like above the tree line? No game, nothing."

He shook his head, then said solemnly, "I keep a fresh coyote hanging in the back at all times for just that kind of emergency."

"Really?"

"No. Bush pilots have a weird sense of humour! It helps."

"Is that why you guys have such funny nicknames?"

"Who've you heard of?"

"Well, 'Black Mac' McDonald, 'Three-Finger' Bob Marten, 'Punch' Dickins, 'Wop' May," I said.

"Yes, I know them — or knew them — all. Their nicknames are well earned."

"Do you have one?"

"Some of the boys call me Midnight."

"How come?"

"Some pilots won't fly at night. Can't see. There's running lights but maybe no landing lights. You've got

to have a feel for where the ground starts, especially
when it's snowing. Sometimes you're on floats and have
to make an emergency landing. You need good eyes, and
a bit of luck."

"And you're good at it?"

"You have to know where the rocks or snags are, be
able to see them, or have a feel for 'em. Someone might
light bonfires on the shoreline, north and south, or
maybe on the other side if they can get across. The
landing doesn't have to be perfect, but it does have to be
safe. And they are. Most of the time."

"Midnight Smith," I said. "Wow. Can I see your pilot's
licence?"

He took a leather wallet from his pocket and showed
me his commercial pilot's licence with the diagonal
green stripe across it. Matthew Cunningham Smith.

"That's my middle name, too," I said.

"Our mother's — your grandmother's — maiden name.
"Dad was named after a fur trader."

"Old Jedediah of the Rocky Mountain Fur Trading
company. Murdered by Indians on the Santa Fe Trail."
Uncle Matthew smiled. "Our family's been around."

"I was born in Dawson City, Yukon. That makes me
a Canadian, like Mom."

"Oh yeah? How come Dawson?"

"There were doctors and a hospital in Dawson City,
so Mom went to stay with Grandma and Grandpa when
I was born. I was a month old when we went back to
Eagle. Dad had a gold claim there."

"So I heard," Uncle Matthew said.

I didn't tell him that when I was four the police came
to Eagle to take Dad away. Mom and I returned to
Grandma and Grandpa's in Dawson City. Dad came and
got us when I was six, and we moved to Fairbanks. I
never knew why he was taken away.

When the storm finally blew out, Dad and I helped Uncle Matthew dig his airplane out of the drifts. We had to tie ropes to the tail and pull back and forth to joggle the skis loose of the snow.

"I'll be back in February to let you know if the high-way deal goes through," Uncle Matthew told Dad. "You ready to leave by March?"

"Guess so. Jay and I'll pull the traps, have the fur bundled." Dad looked anxious, like he was trying to figure a way out of the fix he'd found himself in. Mom was banging pots around in the kitchen to let us know she wasn't happy. I knew now we'd be leaving this place, leaving the best home I'd ever had. We'd be going into Canada. I was sorry to leave but excited, too!

I counted the days until Uncle Matthew would be coming for us: ninety at most. It was a long time to wait.

4

A Bottle Full of Bones

On Christmas Eve we cut down one of the spruce that
grew by the hundreds outside our door and decorated it
with popcorn strings, bells, and candles. Dad, Mom, and
I sat up late talking about the last three years in this
cabin. We had thought we'd stay for a few more years,
but now even Mom had started packing some stuff for
the move. She really had no choice.

At ten o'clock I went out to check on the dogs. As I
gave Conda a good-night pat, I looked back at the cabin.
In the moonlight the scene resembled a Christmas card.
An eighteen-inch blanket of snow covered the gable and
eaves, supported by huge icicles that hung to the
ground. The candles on the Christmas tree shone
through the frosted windowpane. I walked back slowly,
the snow crunching under my boots. A wolf howled from
across the river, and our dogs chorused back.

In the morning we opened our gifts. I gave Mom and
Dad fancy beaded gloves an Indian neighbour had made
from a deerskin I'd tanned. Mom gave Dad and me
hand-knit jumbo sweaters. Dad gave Mom a jacket he'd

had made from the softest deerskin I'd ever seen. He'd built Jody a dollhouse and carved a set of wooden people to live in it. Then he gave me my gift — a new over-and-under rifle, a .22, 410. It was a great little bush gun. The .22 was good for squirrels, rabbits, and rodents, and the 410 perfect for bird hunting. Two guns in one.

Mr. and Mrs. Mackenzie, who ran the trading post thirty miles upriver, came by dogsled to celebrate Christmas with us. Mr. Mackenzie was a big man, over six feet tall and two hundred pounds. He was completely bald except for a raging red beard and always wore a wool toque, a plaid shirt, and big blue overalls. Mrs. Mackenzie was a good match for him in size, and her laughter never ended, just rolled on like spring thunder.

When they arrived, they brought the latest news from overseas. It seemed strange to be sitting in our peaceful wilderness cabin hearing that Germany and Italy had declared war on the United States, and we had turned around and declared war on them.

"Hitler blames the U.S. for starting the war," Mr. Mackenzie informed us. "Says that former president Wilson deceived Germany. So now the fuhrer — that's Hitler — won't have anything to do with President Roosevelt."

I looked at the map tacked to the wall and tried to figure out just where the fighting was the worst. This war was being fought on so many fronts it was hard to keep track. There were pins showing the Allies fighting in Japan, China, Russia, Britain, France, Germany, Italy, and Manila. And now Japanese war planes had been sighted over the American and Canadian west coast!

"Christmas messages will be broadcast tomorrow from the King, President Roosevelt, and Mr. Churchill," Mrs. Mackenzie said. "We'll leave early so we can catch them on our radio at home."

"I guess we'll hear all there is to hear soon enough." For once, Dad seemed regretful that we didn't have a radio. "Now, let's celebrate Christmas. We don't know when we'll have another here."

After our caribou roast dinner we played games — Chinese checkers, Parchesi, Snakes and Ladders, and cards.

"How are you getting along with your school lessons?" Mrs. Mackenzie asked, eyeing my pile of schoolbooks. Since they ran the post office as well as the trading post, they saw my new lessons come in by mail and my completed ones go out every month.

"Okay, I guess. It's kind of boring, sometimes."

"You need to be around other kids more," Mrs. Mackenzie said. "It must be lonely here for a boy your age."

I nodded. I had started school in Fairbanks and made lots of friends there. We'd played baseball and hockey, built forts in the bush and pretended we were soldiers guarding them. I was good at drawing animals because they'd been more a part of my life than people. I got good marks for writing stories, too. Dad usually said something like, "You're getting too smart for your britches!" But I'd catch him reading my stories, his lips moving to say the words silently.

When I was in fifth grade, Dad leased a trapline on the Tanana River. "There's good prices for furs," he said. "If I have to live in town much longer, I'll shoot myself. Always having to look over my shoulder." No one asked him what he meant, and Dad never explained himself.

Mom and I moved to the trapline with him, building a home cabin and fixing up a couple of line cabins along the tributaries to the main river. At first I hated being alone, having no kids to hang around with.

"But you're getting a special kind of education here," Mrs. Mackenzie went on, "seeing nature firsthand. Like town kids never do."

I guess she meant that by being a trapper's son, I got used to seeing death. But I didn't think I ever would take it casually. Nothing dies easily.

Trapping season runs from about October to March. Our area had bear, wolf, coyote, mink, marten, fox, fisher, and beaver. Sometimes I'd go with Dad to lay or check the traps. We travelled with the dogs and stayed in the line cabins, cooking bannock and bacon for supper and drinking tea. But most often I stayed home to look after Mom and Jody. I had lots to do — split wood, carry water, stretch hides . . . and always schoolwork.

When the Mackenzies were ready to leave the day after Christmas, we hitched up our dogs and travelled a few miles with them. Dad and I ran behind the toboggan, Dad holding on to the trailer rope, Mom and Jody bundled up in their parkas and mukluks in the sleigh. The sun sparkled off the crystal-clean snow, and I had to squint to keep out the blinding whiteness. The dogs yipped and yapped, lunging into their harnesses. After about an hour we reached the river and stopped to say good-bye.

Then we called out "Merry Christmas!" and "Happy New Year!" turned our team in a big arc, and headed home.

Before supper, Dad and I went out to check on the dogs and bring in some feed to make into mash for the morning. I watched Dad's shadow play on the shed wall. His shadow arm reached out, long and skinny, and bent to follow the slanted roof line. Looking at him, I saw he'd reached up to take the dog-food bucket from a nail on the wall.

"I wish Uncle Matthew was coming for us right now," I said. "I want him to teach me all about flying."

"So he's your hero now, is he?" The expression on Dad's face hardened.

"He's great! He said he'd — "

Suddenly Dad swung the bucket down from the nail, striking the doorframe with it. The clatter seemed to set him off. Within two minutes he'd cleaned out the shed — all the buckets were thrown out the door and the feed bags, flung like pillows against the wall, were split open, their contents all over the floor.

I ran out the door. As I neared the cabin, I saw my snowshoes on the outside wall. I grabbed them and headed for the bush. When the snow got deep, I put them on and continued with long strides, hardly breaking my speed.

Night falls early in the North in winter, but with moonlight reflecting off the snow, it's often easier to see at night than in the daytime. I headed up an old trail leading to the south end of Dad's trapline. I knew my way, or thought I did. I'd stay overnight in his old line cabin. I wouldn't go back!

After a couple of miles I stopped for breath. Silence surrounded me. I looked around to get my bearings. That clump of spruce on the hillside and the mountain shaped like a buffalo hump looked familiar. I was okay. In fact, Dad had a trap just by those spruce. I went over to it. The trap was still set, and nothing was in it, but a glimmer of glass nearby caught my eye. I dug it out of the snow. It was an old bourbon bottle. Bits of fur clung to the top.

I scraped the frost from the bottle and saw it was full of little skeletons. They looked like mice, but I knew they were shrews — a trapper's worst enemy. They attack the animal in the trap and burrow up the hind end, eating the animal from the inside. Then the hair falls out of the pelt, ruining it. Although they're one of the smallest known mammals, shrews eat three times their weight every day.

I'd seen Dad put a piece of meat into the bottle and set it on an angle. It was easy to figure out what had happened: the first shrew had gone in, slid down the bottle, and ate the meat but couldn't run up the glass to get out. The second went in with the smell of the first one as bait. He'd eaten it, then become bait for the third, and so on. I shook the bottle. The bones clattered softly, like a baby's rattle. There were about a dozen skeletons — a good harvest. The tiny skulls had wide-open jawbones ridged with needle-sharp brown teeth. People sure were the bosses of this world.

I heard a crash back in the trees, and Conda bounded up to me. Then came the slap-slap of snowshoes. I turned away, still holding the bottle. Dad stopped a few feet away.

"I hate shrews," he said, panting.

I held my breath a moment, then let it out in a frosty snort.

"What happened in Eagle?"

"It's not your business to know."

I still couldn't turn around. I didn't want to see his eyes. "Maybe not then," I said, "but it is now."

"I did two years in prison." His voice was real quiet, his breathing still quick from chasing after me. "Jail! It nearly made me crazy. Can't live around people the same. But I'd do it again. Even though it cost me . . . everything."

He wasn't talking to me now. He was talking to Conda, to the shadows ahead of us, the black outlines of the spruce trees, the forest and mountains that went on for hundreds and hundreds of miles.

"When I came out of there, I'd lost my gold claim. Everything. Just your mother stuck by me. If it wasn't for her, I'd have gone out of my head."

I turned to face him. His eyes looked like dark holes in the dusky light.

"What did you do?"

"Got rid of a shrew." He bent to adjust a snowshoe,

and I could barely hear his words. "A man came into the Eagle valley. Robbed miners and trappers of their life's savings. Tricked them out of their pokes. A shyster — no more respect for his fellow man than those things in the bottle."

"What did you do to him?"

"Burned him out. It was against the law, and I paid. But I'd do it again. He left the North. But if I ever run into Braden again, he'll wish he — "

"He's gone?"

"He threatened to pay me back, burn me, but I'll kill him first. Told him. You coming?"

"Yeah." I tossed the bottle full of bones into the snow.

The moon lay in a silver path from the edge of the lake to our camp. The Northern Lights had started throwing faint green ripples across the sky.

Conda barked our return, and Mom opened the cabin door to tell us we were late for supper. We headed toward the bright rectangle of light. I knew Dad would never say any more about the shrew from Eagle.

I lay in bed that night, listening to homey sounds — logs settling, clock ticking, Jody babbling in her sleep. The inside of the cabin was pitch black, the only light coming from a red line around the edge of the stove door, where the coals were slowly dying. I thought about the Christmas we'd just celebrated, how peaceful it had been here before we'd heard about America being in the war. Before Uncle Matthew had zoomed in, blowing our lives wide open.

I wished I could hear President Roosevelt and Mr. Churchill and the King give their Christmas speeches on the radio. I wished I could discuss things with someone my age who shared the same feelings I had. Maybe even a girl. I wished I could spend more time with Uncle Matthew and learn about my Grandpa Smith, who I'd never met.

I wished I could talk more with Dad, ask him abou[t] when he was growing up, if he remembered what it wa[s] like to be crazy with wanting something but not knowin[g] what it was, feeling a little bit scared and a little bi[t] angry and a little bit wild. I bet he'd know.

The bottle full of bones told more than one story.

5

Fire and Ice

Uncle Matthew flew back at the end of February with
news: a man named Otto Knapp wanted Dad to come
and run his sawmill near Fort St. John, B.C.

"An official order to begin work on the supply road
went through on February fourteenth," Uncle Matthew
told us. "Valentine's Day. Good omen, wouldn't you say?"

"They starting at Dawson Creek?" Dad asked.

"That will be the official Mile Zero. The road will run
through Canada, then up to the Richardson Highway at
Delta Junction and from there to Fairbanks. But I think
they're planning to build it in sections. There'll be crews
working from one end to the other."

"Who's footing the bill for all this?"

"A cost-sharing deal between the American and Canadian governments. The Americans are supplying
troops and equipment. Canadians are giving the okay
for the road to be built through B.C. and the Yukon. No

import duties, sales tax, or income tax. No immigratio
regulations. And they're throwing in the gravel, timbe
and rock from government land along the route."

"As Americans, does it matter where we work?" Da
sounded more excited now. I avoided looking at Mom.

"Jed, you and I — and Jay — are going to work fron
one end of this cotton-pickin' road to the other! In th
air, in the bush, on the road — who cares? They'r
paying big bucks for long hours. The U.S. has budgete
a billion dollars a week on the war effort for 1942! We'r
going to win this war, and quickly!"

Then Uncle Matthew turned to me. "By the time thi
road's laid out, you'll be a match for any man in th
North. You'll get all the ABCs you'll ever need, righ
here."

"Six months, and that's it." Mom's voice was quiet, bu
we could hear her all right. "By fall we're back here, an
Jay will be boarded in Fairbanks, enrolled in high
school. Jay's studies will *not* be traded for some back
breaking bush work."

"That's right, Lilly," Dad said. "And the money w
make building the highway's going to pay to put hin
there."

We pulled our traps the first week of March, and Uncle
Matthew flew in again on the tenth. He had more news
about the highway: the first detachment of U.S. military
engineers — five officers and 127 enlisted men — had
arrived in Dawson Creek, B.C. The weather was thirty
below.

Dad went out with Uncle Matthew, taking along his
winter fur catch and some of our household stuff, including Mom's harmonium. Dad hugged us all in turn. "I
hate leaving you here," he said, "but I have to get started
on the job and find us a place to live."

"I'll be back in five days," Uncle Matthew said, as he prepared for takeoff. "Take good care of the ladies, Jay."

Taking care of the ladies turned out to be more than I'd expected. Mom wasn't acting normal. I'd hear her crying in the night sometimes, and during the day she seemed withdrawn and forgetful. She burned three batches of cookies one after the other. I tried to talk about the war, but she just said, "Men!"

"Uncle Matthew might teach me to fly, Mom," I said, trying another topic.

"If God wanted you to have wings, he'd have glued a pair onto your back."

Hmmm. Another try. "It will be nice for you to have company at the sawmill. Maybe there'll be other women there for you to visit with."

"I've never missed gossip," she said.

"Well, Dad seems kind of excited about it."

She looked at me, her violet eyes filling with tears. "Oh, Jay. You don't know — his temper — I don't want him back in civilization."

We ended up playing cards, but it was like playing with Jody. I won every game.

On the fifteenth of March we started listening for the sound of the Norseman, but none came.

"I'm going to make a couple of pies," Mom said on the seventeenth. "We can take them with us." She set some frozen bear grease on the back of the stove to warm up while we went outside to clean the old shed. Jody came with us, as Mom would never leave her inside the house alone. The snow had started to melt a bit, but there were still several inches on the ground. At this time of year, we could get another storm any time.

When the shed was straightened out, I went to chop wood. Mom set Jody on the woodpile, then grabbed a hatchet and began to split some kindling. I looked over at the cabin. A beautiful orange sun was reflecting in the window.

But there was no sun today!

"Fire!" I screamed as I raced toward the cabin. Mom threw Jody into the shed, shut the door, and ran after me.

I yanked open the cabin door. A wall of flame roared up from the stove. The heat protector, a metal-covered sheet of asbestos, glowed red and bulged with heat. I grabbed a bucket of water from beside the door and threw it onto the flames. A cloud of hissing steam shot up, blinding me. Sparks showered the checkered curtain around the bottom cupboard, and it became a line of fire.

"Jay, watch out!" Mom screamed.

I struck at the flames with a blanket, but there was fire everywhere. Mom dunked a towel into the wash basin, and holding it over her nose and eyes, ran back to the bedroom. "Come back, Mom!" I yelled.

In the distance I could hear Jody wailing in the shed and the dogs howling. I was choking and crying now as I beat and beat at the fire. It was no use.

I grabbed my new gun from the wall and threw some ammunition into my pocket. I looked around quickly to see what else we should take, and grabbed some sleeping bags. Then Mom was beside me again, her black hair in her eyes, soot streaked across her face.

"Mom, let's go!" I tried to catch her arm, but she ran behind me, grabbing the pot of stew, the picture of her parents from the mantle. She seemed to be searching for something else as I pushed her out the door. "The letters!" she cried, but I held her back.

Mom and I stood by the shed, holding a sobbing Jody and watching our little house burn. Even the dogs just sat quietly. When the house collapsed, it threw up chips of wood, bits of papery things, and sparks that soared into the winter sky.

I had a vision of the shrews. Braden's threat! This was it! But it couldn't have been Braden. I'd have seen his tracks, and the dogs would have caught his scent. Still, I decided to check for tracks later.

My throat hurt from screaming, and my eyes burned from rubbing them with my soot-stained hands. The dogs began to whimper. I looked around. We couldn't use the storage shed for shelter because it was too small to contain a camp fire. Sleeping bags and our parkas were all we had to protect us from the sub-zero temperatures.

Mom held Jody and stroked her back, murmuring, "It's over, hush dear, it's over."

"Uncle Matthew will be here tomorrow for sure," I said.

She looked at the lead-coloured sky but said nothing.

I built a fire, though it seemed stupid building one when just a hundred feet away our house lay smouldering. But we didn't dare go near it — there was ammunition in the house, and it could still go off in the hot ashes. Mom pulled an old bear hide from the shed for us to sit on. She rocked Jody while she looked at the picture she'd rescued.

"Mom, what letters were you looking for?"

"Your dad — "

"Love letters?"

"He ordered curtains for his cabin at Eagle. I was working for my parents in Dawson City at the trading post. I made him two sets, red-checkered."

"Dad ordered curtains?"

"I thought he was some toothless old miner losing his marbles out in the bush."

Something exploded into a shower of flames — maybe the kerosene lamps. She watched, then continued.

"Another letter came. He wanted a tablecloth — with lace."

"Lace?"

"Lace! What next? A crocheted bedspread?" She laughed, choking on the smoke. I waited until she'd caught her breath. "Then one day he walked into the store and ordered me to marry him."

"Just like Dad! You'd never seen him before?"

"No. But he stayed around town long enough to convince me he was the one."

We both stared at the smouldering mess.

"We've had a pretty good life here, up to now, haven't we, Mom?"

Mom nodded, tears streaking slowly down her soot-covered cheeks.

Night fell, brightened by the still-glowing coals of the cabin. As there wasn't much else to do, we crawled into our sleeping bags to keep warm. I felt completely exhausted, but the staccato sound of bullets popping like fireworks scared away any thoughts of sleep.

Mom rolled over. "Are you all right, Jay?"

"Yeah, Mom, don't worry."

But I didn't feel all right at all. Where was Uncle Matthew? Had the shrew set the fire? Was Dad's job working out? If it wasn't, we had absolutely nowhere to go.

I lay listening to the wolves howl in the distance. I didn't know if it was good to be growing up. There were so many responsibilities. Sometimes I felt like a kid and sometimes like a . . . hadn't Uncle Matthew called me a man? Well, sort of, when he'd said the trapline was a great place for a kid but not much for a young man. What was I, anyway? What did you call a guy like me, smart in some ways but dumber than an egg in others? I wondered about the people I'd be meeting down south, how I'd get along with them. How was Dad was getting along with them? That got me so worried I didn't fall asleep until after the wolves did.

During the night, we took turns waking up and

throwing more wood onto the fire. When I awoke for the third time, it was light enough to make out the cache where Dad had stored his pelts. It stood high against the sky, stark in the dim light. I could see the glimmer of the tin plates we'd nailed under the platform at the top ends of the supporting posts to prevent rodents from getting at the furs. I was stiff with cold, and by the way the ice hung in the air, I could tell the temperature was dropping. It would snow for sure.

I got up quietly and took Conda off her chain to help with my detective work. She'd be able to smell tracks that had been covered with a skiff of snow. We circled the camp. Coyote tracks, wolf, moose. But no shrew.

The day slowly got lighter. When I got back to camp, Mom was still sleeping, with Jody curled up against her inside her parka. A lump formed in my throat when I thought how much I loved them, and how scary our situation was — and I was in charge of it.

As I built up the fire and heated the stew, I decided I had to get Mom and Jody to Mackenzie's trading post. When Mom awoke, she agreed. While she fed the dogs, I scrawled a message for my uncle on the shed wall with charcoal.

The ashes had cooled enough so we could poke through the rubble. I used a fishing rod from the shed to hook some pots and cups from the wreckage that had once been our cupboard. Ravens watched us, waiting for the house to cool down so they, too, could salvage. Mom brushed back tears as she looked at the charred remains of the beds, table, and chairs that Dad had made. With my next cast, I pulled up a blackened pot.

"That's the cause of the fire," Mom said. "The bear grease. It must have overheated. It's all my fault."

"I shouldn't have thrown water on it," I said, relieved that the fire had been started by grease, not a shrew.

We stood for a moment, surveying the mess. "I guess

you'll have to sew up some new curtains," I said. "Yellow this time. With lace." Mom laughed, and wiped at her eyes.

I punched holes in a syrup pail, stuck some burning coals inside, and put it in the sleigh. It was our only source of fire. Then Mom and Jody got into the toboggan.

I never had time to say good-bye to our ruined home. I was running to keep up with the dogs.

6

From Dog Runner to Copilot

The dogs headed down the familiar trail, noses down, tail brushes up, and I followed, hanging onto the trailer rope. The snow started coming in gusts, blowing from the north. I turned around for a final look at the camp, but the snow blinded me. With the house gone, it wouldn't take long for the forest to grow back and hide any signs we had ever lived there.

When we got out of the trees and into open country the storm became vicious. The trail was quickly buried in snow, but I wasn't worried about getting lost because once we reached the river the banks would guide us. My only concern then would be the condition of the ice. The river usually stayed frozen a good five months of every year, but it was an uneasy freeze with air holes and broken ice caused by pressure ridges.

I called "Uke!" and the dogs veered to the right, then "Chaw!" and we headed left, the toboggan sliding down the drop to the river. I stopped the dogs, and Mom and Jody got off to stretch their legs while I checked the ice.

"We'll be fighting the wind all the way," Mom said.

Frost balled up on my eyelashes and melted into tears. I took my mitt off to wipe my face and looked north and south, along the river. "We'll make it," I said. "We've gone eight miles — only twenty-two more to go."

The dog-trot of the team seemed slow, but it was actually a mile-eating pace. On a good trek the team averaged eight or ten miles per hour and could go fifty miles a day with no problem. But this was rough going, especially for me, jumping on and off the sled depending on the terrain.

Mom ran with me and the dogs for a while. I didn't feel cold, although the freezing wind and snow stung my eyes, snapped at my cheeks and chin, froze my nose. The dogs were skittish, turning away from the driving snow, resisting my commands. I wondered if we'd make it to Mackenzie's without trouble. When we stopped again I put Shiloh in the lead to give Conda a rest. But Shiloh hated the icy blasts and kept pulling to the left.

We reached one of our line cabins where Bear Creek flowed into the Tanana River. Dad and I often stayed there overnight when we checked the traps. It was small but had a stove. We pulled over for a rest stop. As I filled the little stove with wood to heat the stew and boil some snow for tea, I wondered if we should stay here.

"I think we should camp," Mom said, as if reading my thoughts. "The weather is miserable."

I went to the toboggan for the stew and coals and took them back inside. The coals had gone out. I took my hunting knife, chopped frozen stew out of the pot and ate an icy chunk. It sank like a rock in my stomach. "No thanks," Mom said when I passed a piece over to her. Jody made a face and turned away from it, too, and I could see why. But worse, with no fire we couldn't stay.

Soon we were travelling again. Mom and Jody, facing me in the carry-all, peeked out through their furs. I rode on the back of the toboggan, my feet resting on the flat edge.

Snow pellets were hitting at an angle, and it was hard to keep to the trail. Hummocks of snow and ice caused the toboggan to slide a bit. Then the toboggan slithered sharply, nearly causing Jody to fall off.

Shiloh steered the team over to the edge of the river, and the dogs scrambled wildly to climb the slope. What was the matter with them? And why was Conda following? I stopped the dogs and looked around, squinting into the blinding whiteness. Before us on the river rose a pressure ridge of jumbled ice blocks. The ice had reared up, broken, frozen, then split and refrozen until it formed a row of icebergs across the river.

Mom held the dogs while I went ahead and tested for a crossing place. The ice groaned as if alive. I found a spot that looked strong enough to support our weight. First I took Mom and Jody across, then went back for the dogs. The dark water swirling around rocks under broken shards of ice made them nervous. Brutus, the wheel dog, yelped as his hind quarters broke through. The force of the other dogs scrambling ahead pulled him onto his feet. The toboggan shuddered across the broken surface.

Mom and Jody got back into the sleigh, and again I ran behind. We were over halfway there. The wind let up, but the snow still fell heavily to the ground.

The hours wore on. It seemed that as the snow fell slower, we travelled slower; when dusk fell around five o'clock I wondered if we were moving at all. Soon it would be too dangerous to go on. We'd have to camp and wait until daybreak.

A cold blast of wind cleared the air for a moment; it blew against my face, taking my breath away. Where were we? I knew this river fairly well, but in the storm I couldn't tell whether we'd rounded the bend upriver from Mackenzie's yet. I felt scared. And I was tired, and so hungry I was starting to feel sick.

"Are you all right, Jay?" Mom called.

"I'm fine, Mom."

Then I thought I saw a glimmer of light ahead. I tried to wipe the ice from my lashes, but my moosehide mitts were frozen and rasped across my stiff cheeks. We travelled on another few minutes. Again the wind came up and cleared the snow. There was a light.

"Mom!" I pointed. "Mackenzie's trading post!" The dogs started yapping, and the Mackenzie's dogs answered.

Soon I could see Mrs. Mackenzie standing in the doorway, the light silhouetting her big frame. We pulled up in a whoosh of flying snow. I took Jody from Mom and handed her over to Mrs. Mackenzie's waiting arms. "There was a fire — the cabin burned down!" I panted.

"Oh, my dears! I hope you weren't hurt! Matthew radioed to say he was snowed in and was overdue to get you. But we thought you'd be all right."

I turned to give Mom a hand. When she tried to get up and fell back, I realized what a close call we'd had. I brushed the snow from her parka and helped her out of the toboggan.

"You did it, Jay," she said. "I'm proud of you."

Mr. Mackenzie came into the store from the back, where they lived. "Here, boy, let's get those dogs fed and watered. They can bed out back. And you . . . you need food and water, too!

"Your uncle can't make it until tomorrow at the earliest. I was going to leave in the morning to see how you were doing."

"Not very well, I'm afraid," Mom said. She started to cry.

Mrs. Mackenzie shifted Jody to one arm, took Mom

in her other arm, and hugged them both. "There, there," she said. "You're all right now."

Uncle Matthew flew in two days later, landing on the river ice. He'd had to sit out the storm at Fairbanks. When we told him about losing the house, his face went pale. "Oh God, and you were waiting for me! I'm so sorry."

"Don't feel bad. You told me to take good care of the ladies, so I did!" I smiled and noted his look of relief.

Uncle Matthew had the latest war news, and a lot of it was about the Alaska Highway. "The U.S. has officially offered to construct the highway and maintain it during the war. After that, it will revert to the Dominion of Canada to become part of their highway system."

"Has work actually started yet?" Mr. Mackenzie asked.

"Well, the 35th Engineer Regiment — a bunch of officers and over a thousand enlisted men — just showed up in Dawson Creek with nine hundred tons of supplies. I guess you could call that a serious indication that the job will go ahead!"

We loaded up and left the next day. The dogs whined at being muzzled and tied, but there was no other way to travel with them in the plane. The toboggan was tied under the fuselage, then Mom and Jody squeezed into the cabin. I climbed into the copilot's seat.

My first airplane ride! The Norseman rattled down the ice on its big skis, and in moments we were airborne. The river looked as smooth as a ribbon when in reality it had given us eight hours of misery. In minutes we were over the black smudge in the little clearing that used to be home. I swallowed.

"Tell me about flying, Uncle Matthew."

"Okay. When you learn to fly you start with seven basic principles."

"Hey," Mom said from the back seat, "school again, Jay!"

"You bet! Three movements," Uncle Matthew continued. "Pitch, roll, and yaw. Remember that. And, four attitudes: banked, straight and level, climbing, and descending."

I repeated them.

"You 'roll' an aircraft to a 'banked' attitude. Got it?"

"Huh?"

"An aircraft is rolled to a position where the wings are at an angle to the horizon. When the roll is stopped, you say the aircraft is in a banked attitude. The term 'banking' an aircraft is commonly used, but isn't right."

Uncle Matthew explained the oil pressure and altitude gauges, the rudder and control column. "Looks simple, doesn't it?" he yelled over the roar of the engine. "Here, you take it."

I didn't dare turn around to see Mom's reaction.

"Take the steering column. Hold it steady and watch the horizon to keep level. Watch the altimeter, too, so you'll know if you're going up or down."

My hands sweating, I grabbed the wheel and pulled it toward me. Nellie shot almost straight up.

"Whoa!" Uncle Matthew called. "Push 'er down a bit."

I jammed it back, putting the plane into a dive.

"Jay, level off now!"

I pulled back on the steering column again, not as hard this time, breathing deeply to control my nervousness. My heart was pounding. "Okay! I've got it now!"

I heard only half of what he said because I was trying to think of everything all at once and look at the instruments to see how they reacted to my movements.

"You're way off course to the right!" Uncle Matthew said. "Roll left, but easy does it! Level the wings out now. Good! Hold it there. Good. Now roll back to the right and level out. There we are. Back on course." I was on top of the world.

Uncle Matthew put his hands on the control column. "I have control now," he said. I tried to relax my hands, but I couldn't. I rubbed them together to work out the cramps. One thing for sure, though, I loved flying!

We flew on for about another half-hour. As we crossed the border from Alaska into the Yukon territory, my uncle pointed out landmarks I'd only heard about — the White and Donjek rivers, the St. Elias Mountains, the Kluane ranges and Kluane Lake, the old trading post of Champagne . . . but then he became preoccupied with the gauges.

I wasn't sure, but I thought the sound of the engine was changing. Uncle Matthew kept looking out the window. His face was like granite, so I didn't ask him any more questions.

He turned to me. "I think I might have to put her down for a minute."

"Why?"

"We've been losing power for the last fifteen, twenty miles. I don't know if it's the magnetos, carburettor ice, or ice in the fuel line. Don't worry, it'll just be a normal landing like any other time. But it might be a good idea if you tell your mom we're going to set down."

I looked back at Mom. She already knew something was wrong.

"Might be carb-ice," my uncle said. "I'm trying Carb-Heat. If it doesn't clear right away, we're putting down." He fiddled with a switch. Nothing changed. "Better land while I still have power and control, rather than waiting up here to see if it gets worse.

"We just passed a long narrow lake. We're going back to it. It's the only clear spot I can see."

Then he picked up the microphone. "This is Norseman November Charlie one-nine-five November. Making emergency landing west end of Blight Lake. Losing power. Will call again after landing. Over."

He waited a few seconds; there was no reply. Uncle Matthew broadcast the same message again. Still no reply. Turning to me he said, "Tighten your seat belt. Tell your mother to do the same." I did. I was now frozen to my seat. We began a long gentle turn toward the lake below.

"This wind is stronger than I thought," he added. "We're going to be short, but we'll just make it over the trees."

There was a loud whumph! whumph! like we were being smacked by a large broom as the skis hit the tops of several trees. When we were clear of the trees, Uncle Matthew dived the plane just a little and levelled out. "You should always land into the wind. A bird won't even land downwind. But this time, we are."

"Why?"

"So we'll bounce over the hard snowdrifts. Water only flows one way, wind can come from any direction. Look at the curl on those drifts. And they'll be hard as rocks."

The crusted snowdrifts rippled across the lake in a series of waves. It was easy to see that if we'd landed the other way, our skis would have caught the curled-over points of the drifts, and we might have somersaulted the airplane.

Tail down, we made a three-point landing on the wheel at the back and the skis underneath, and settled onto the white surface of the frozen lake. He switched off the engine and closed the throttle. Finally we came to a stop, and everything was very quiet. Uncle Matthew turned to me. "Not bad for no brakes!"

I looked at Mom. She was sitting absolutely still, holding Jody in her arms, her teeth chattering so hard I could hear them.

"We're down, Lil. I think I can figure out what's wrong pretty quick. We're safe and that's the main thing."

I looked out at the bleak surroundings.

"I try to land as near as possible to the west or north shorelines, then park with the tail as close to shoreline as I can get it."

"How come?"

"Windbreak. Also," Uncle Matthew pointed toward some scruffy brush sticking out of the snow on the shore, "more firewood. The best firewood is found on the south side of a slope, which is right next to you if you've landed on the north end of a lake. And smoke drifts away from the machine . . . and heat radiates back under the tarp."

"Firewood?" Mom's voice was really quiet. "Yes. We've got to get a fire going. There's some dead trees . . . but the snow will be too deep."

"That's why I always carry snowshoes. Axe. File. Survival gear." He laughed, and assumed a drawl, "This ain't my first rodeo, Lilly-May!"

Mom smiled, too.

On landing we'd broken a strut that held on a ski, but Uncle Matthew wasn't too concerned about that. "I can fix it with a wood splint and moosehide or rope," he said casually. "It will do for at least one takeoff and one landing."

But what had happened to the engine?

Uncle Matthew removed the cowling and after several minutes he found the problem. "Ice in the fuel line. Wouldn't think a little pellet of ice no bigger than an eraser on a pencil could bring an airplane down, would you? The only way we're going to melt it out is by putting a tarpaulin over the engine and lighting a small fire."

We brought the dogs out, unmuzzled them, and tied them to the ski struts. I put on the snowshoes and headed across the snow to gather some wood. We were lucky that there was some.

Mom unwrapped the turkey sandwiches Mrs. Mackenzie had packed for us and made tea by melting a pot of snow over the fire we built. "Good thing it's not too cold," she commented. "Must be just a bit below zero."

Uncle Matthew tried the radio again, but there was still no reply. "I don't know if they got our message or not."

We draped the tarp over the engine like a tent, and in no time it was warm as toast inside. "Got to be careful doing this," said my uncle. "More than one airplane has been set on fire trying to fix this problem!"

When the engine had heated, he uncoupled the fuel line to make sure the gas was flowing.

After we'd eaten, Uncle Matthew and I went to work fixing the broken strut, lashing it with wooden sticks and one of the dog harnesses. We cleared a runway strip on the lake as best we could, then taxied around until we got into position.

"Well, that's it," he said. "Let's give it a try."

He fired up the engine and just as we were preparing for takeoff, we saw a low-flying airplane coming straight at us, rocking its wings, from the north end of the long lake. It whooshed overhead. Uncle Matthew grabbed his microphone and called over the radio. "November Charlie one-nine-five November. We're okay, frozen fuel line, frozen passengers. Repeat, we're okay. Retain visual contact until we are airborne. Over." There was a crackling, garbled sound from the other pilot: "Wilco, November Charlie one-nine-five November. Good luck! Weather clear to Whitehorse. Out."

The airplane had turned around and was coming back low. As it flashed by I could see the pilot's face looking down at us. I waved and he rocked his wings.

For a moment I wasn't on the ground; I was that pilot, looking down.

Uncle Matthew revved up the engine. "Looks like we're back in business. Hang on. It's going to be rough getting out of here." We roared across the ice, thumping and bumping, and then suddenly the jolting stopped and we were free and clear in smooth air. The other airplane joined up, and we flew in formation. I could see the pilot all the time.

We stopped in Whitehorse for repairs and sent a message down to Dad that we'd been delayed.

"Don't tell your Dad about the cabin," Mom warned me. "I'll handle that."

The other pilot left us in Whitehorse, and we continued along the Northwest Staging Route, which Uncle Matthew had helped set up, to Watson Lake, Yukon. On our way south over the Rocky Mountains to Fort Nelson, B.C., Uncle Matthew pointed out the great Liard River, which the Alcan would follow for many miles.

"That's the Smith River down there and the falls."

"Named after us?"

Uncle Matthew smiled. "I like to think it was." He pointed upriver. "To the north, about twenty miles up Teeter Creek, is a place it's best to steer clear of called the Valley of Lost Planes . . . or Million Dollar Valley . . . take your pick."

"How come?"

"Downdrafts throw you around pretty bad, can toss you to the ground. A million dollars worth of aircraft wrecked in there. It's wrecked some people, too."

A shiver ran down my spine as I looked toward the valley, but clouds hid it from view.

At Fort Nelson war planes were lined up at the airfield. "They're P-40 fighter planes — Curtiss-Warhawks,"

Uncle Matthew told me. "All ready for war against Japanese bombers."

They were huge, fierce-looking planes. I thought of the brave men who'd be flying them into combat. Oh, boy, I wanted to fly!

We flew on to Charlie Lake near Fort St. John, our final destination.

Dad and his boss, Otto Knapp, met us with a team of horses and a sleigh to take us to the sawmill. I ran up to Dad. "We had the best trip! All over the country!" A look passed between Dad and Mom, and I decided to keep the rest for later. Dad went to Mom, hugging her hard.

"The house burned, Jed," Mom said. She started to sob.

"Oh Lilly!"

"A pot of grease — my fault! I should have known better. But, I'm glad it was only that. Not him."

"Sshhh. You're safe now. We're all together and we're going to stay that way."

"Yes, we're here now," Mom said, her voice strong again. "There's no going back."

I was shocked to hear that Mom had maybe shared my fears about the shrew setting the fire. Did she know I knew about him?

"You folks have a lot of catching up to do," Uncle Matthew said after he'd helped us unload our stuff. "I've got to go on to Edmonton and get Nellie overhauled." He turned to me. "I'll take you flying again when I get back, Jay."

"That's great!" I said, but Dad interrupted.

"The kid's working. School lessons. Helping his mother. Driving skid horses, tailing at the mill. He's got no time for flying around like a . . . a playboy."

I heard Uncle Matthew suck in his breath. I looked

down at my mukluks. The wind was sharper here, with a bite that told me that, although we were a thousand miles farther south, it was still North country, and March was still a lion. Something like my Dad.

"Whatever you say, Jed." Uncle Matthew shook Mom's and my hands, then stood before Dad. Dad coughed, looked away red-faced, then stuck out his hand. "Thanks for bringing my family out, Matt. I'll pay you when I get some cash."

"No need. Call it my contribution to the war effort."

I walked Uncle Matthew back to his airplane, although I couldn't think of anything to say, and watched him taxi away, then climb into the sky. He dipped his wings in farewell before turning south toward Alberta.

I looked at Otto Knapp's team of horses, a matched pair of big blacks with slashes of white down their foreheads. They were beautiful, but so big! They tossed their heads and turned back to see what we were loading.

"Satin and Silky." Mr. Knapp grabbed the bridle of the one nearest him. The horse tossed its big head, nearly pulling Mr. Knapp up with him. "Silky's quiet; Satin's the feisty one. You're going to have to watch him. This is the team you'll be driving."

"Jay's going to be driving these beasts?" Mom said, coming up behind me.

"I thought you said the boy could handle it," Mr. Knapp said to Dad, then he spit a wad of tobacco onto the ground and rubbed it into the snow with his boot.

"He can, and he will."

"Well, Jay, you're the newest man on the payroll," Mr. Knapp said.

I wasn't a kid anymore — I was a grown-up, the newest man on the payroll. I'd be driving these skid horses by myself. Tailing, too, whatever that was. I went up to Silky with my hand extended. She shoved her nose down into my moosehide mitt, then flipped her head up. I figured she liked me. I'd just have to learn their habits, figure them out. If I was the newest man on the payroll, I'd have to learn to survive in a man's world. Avoiding Mom's eyes, I turned and spit onto the packed snow.

7

The Shaganappi Sawmill

"I've been preaching for a long time to these
boys in congress and the war department that
if we are going to win this war we'd better do it
through Alaska."

— Anthony Dimond,
Alaskan Delegate to the U.S.

I drove the team into camp with Mr. Knapp sitting next
to me instructing me how to handle the horses. Mom,
Dad, and Jody sat in the back of the sleigh on top of our
gear. The dogs were tied behind. As we approached the
camp we saw piles of logs stacked everywhere. A saw
was screaming nonstop, and the smell of fresh sawdust
hung in the air.

"We've got contracts for every size of wood we can
throw through the saws," Mr. Knapp shouted over the
scream of machinery. "The 'gummint' wants this road
through yesterday! And everything's top secret — the
whole project. We're in a war, boy," he said, apparently
for my benefit. "Every able-bodied man has joined the
forces, leaving old duffers like your dad and me — and
young squirts like you — to look after defence at home.

Kids and old farts to save the home turf!" He threw back his head and laughed through snuff-stained teeth.

Otto Knapp was a big man with a pot belly, a red face, and eyes to match. His whiskers made him resemble a fat badger. "Yep, this war will be won by the man behind the man behind the gun, and don't you forget it. People at home producing everything. Food. Airplanes. Paying taxes and buying war bonds. And building this godforsaken road."

The president of the United States had ordered the Army to get the Alcan Highway punched through the bush as quickly as possible. The southern headquarters of the project was in Fort St. John, the northern headquarters in Whitehorse. Troops that had just come in by train to Dawson Creek were put to work right away getting supplies to camp sites up along the trapper's trail from Dawson Creek to Fort Nelson before the spring thaw. Otto Knapp had contracts to supply wood for building those camps and for firewood. Later, he hoped to get contracts for bridge materials.

Knapp's sawmill was set up a few miles northwest of Charlie Lake. It was one of the most shaganappi outfits I'd ever seen. That's a word Dad uses to describe something that's held together by baling wire and hope, using every shortcut and cheap system possible. Mr. Knapp looked at the mill like a king surveying his realm.

In a clearing were seven tents on wooden platforms. Mr. Knapp pointed to a long skid shack, which was just a cheaply-built house on logs or skids so it could be hauled to another location, and announced that it was the dining hall. Stuck back in the trees were two smaller skid shacks. One was where Mr. Knapp and his wife lived. He told me to pull the team up in front of the other.

"Home sweet home," he said jovially to Mom. "There's enough furniture in there to get you by." He hopped off the sleigh and offered Mom his hand. She hesitated, then took it.

We unloaded our gear, and I started to get off the sleigh, but Mr. Knapp stopped me. "Here, boy." He handed me the reins. "Take 'em away to the barn."

Mom whirled on him. "Jay is not driving those horses by himself!"

"Well, now." Mr. Knapp's face turned storm dark. "Hey, Jed! Is this here boy of yours able to do a day's work, or am I going to have to hire me a water boy?" he yelled over to Dad, who was busy tying the dogs to trees around our shack. They were going crazy, barking their heads off at the camp dogs, adding to the ear-splitting noise of the sawmill.

Dad came walking back, his eyes stony. "He'll do the job, Otto. But someone's got to take him around a bit first. He isn't too used to horses."

I sure wasn't. There weren't many horses back in the bush in Alaska. They didn't winter very well at sixty below zero.

Mr. Knapp stood with the reins in his hand. I climbed on the sleigh and took them from him. I heard Mom gasp, but I didn't look at her. "Go on, Jay," Dad said.

I flipped the reins a bit, as I'd seen Mr. Knapp do, and the team started up.

"Gee!" Mr. Knapp yelled, and they turned to the right. I held the reins firmly, feeling more confident now. If I could manage four unruly dogs, I could surely handle two well-trained horses.

I took them over to a shack that served as the barn, then jumped down and helped Mr. Knapp unhitch the horses from the sleigh. We led them inside where they stood quietly, tossing their heads as I slipped off the heavy bridles, complete with leather eyeshades called blinders. They were each given a half-pail of oats and some hay.

"They're good animals," Mr. Knapp said, as he brushed Satin. "Treat 'em fair, and they'll work their tails off for you." Their ears twitched to our voices.

I brushed Silky, feeling her hard muscles ripple under my hands. I didn't care what jobs Mr. Knapp and Dad had me doing at this shaganappi sawmill — as long as I could work with the horses.

Our shack had one room. The plain board walls were laced silver with frost. Two sets of bunks were nailed to opposite walls behind a wooden table and four chairs, and the heater was a forty-five-gallon drum set on its side, with legs and a stove pipe fitted onto it. That was our home. No curtains, not a scrap of linoleum on the floor, no cupboards, nothing.

As soon as we had the fire going, Mom unpacked the stuff Uncle Matthew had brought from the home cabin. She and Dad strung sheets on wire to give some privacy around the bunk beds. Then she unrolled her rag rugs, flung a tablecloth over the scarred table, and suddenly we had a not-bad place.

At six o'clock we went over to the mess hall for supper — we would be eating with the crew because there wasn't a cookstove in our house. The camp cook was a big man nicknamed Muskwa. That meant "bear" in Cree, and he sure resembled a bear, in his looks and gruff manner.

Muskwa had stacked enamel bowls near the stove so they'd be warm when he ladled food into them. We sat at one end of the long oilcloth-covered table. Ten men came in, ranging in age from their teens to their sixties. Nobody removed his hat, just flipped up ear-flaps, or pushed back parka hoods. Gloves were taken off only to break burnt chunks of bread into bowls. The men were bearded, and had shaggy hair. Some had no teeth, or pulled a set out of their pockets to eat with. A couple of them nodded toward Mom, Jody, and me, touched fingers to caps in a kind of salute, then turned full attention to their food.

We looked down at the stew that Muskwa had slopped into our bowls. Mom turned pale.

"It doesn't taste that bad, Lilly," Dad said. "He just throws a bit of everything into the pot and prays."

"Prays for what — that we don't all die?" I said, dipping my spoon into the stew. "Why is it pink?"

Mom tasted it. "It's got beets in it, that's why. We can't eat this."

"Why don't you be the cook, Mom?"

Otto Knapp sat down beside us. "How's the grub?"

"Awful!" I said.

"You could use another cook," Dad said.

"Ha! Try to find one. Either they can't boil water without burning it, or they're drunk all the time," Mr. Knapp said.

"I can cook." We all looked at Mom. "And I don't drink. I wouldn't mind hiring on as Muskwa's helper."

"Too many men in camp," Dad replied curtly. "Some of 'em running from the law — U.S. and Canadian. Best avoid them all you can."

Mom gave him a funny look. "Yes, I wouldn't want to get mixed up with any man who's ever had trouble with the law," she said quietly.

Dad looked away. "Fine. Go ahead. But if there's any trouble, I'll beat the guy's head in. Count on it."

Mr. Knapp dropped his spoon into his grey-looking coffee, making it slop over onto the tablecloth.

"I can bake anything you want and feed five or fifty." There was a short silence. "And I'd want the same money you're paying your mill hands."

"But . . . you're a woman!" Mr. Knapp said. Mom looked him right in the eye. "I mean . . . we don't have any women working in this camp. The men may not like it."

"I want her." Muskwa stood at the end of our table, a

long kitchen knife in his hand. Now I knew another reason for his name — he smelled like a bear, too. Mom stared back at Mr. Knapp.

"Okay then. Start tomorrow morning, five o'clock. Muskwa will have the fire going. Do whatever he tells you."

Mom smiled up at Muskwa, and the big man's face burst into a relieved grin. His bushy mustache lifted to reveal two gleaming gold teeth. He transferred the knife to his left hand and held his right hand out to Mom. "A deal," Mom said to Mr. Knapp, and shook Muskwa's hairy paw.

Jody was picking little rock-like raisins out of her pudding. "Well, kid," I said, "looks like you're the only one in the family who's not making a buck pushing this road through."

"Give her a year," Mom said, laughing. It was good to hear Mom laugh.

On the way out of the mess hall, we looked at the big thermometer hanging on the outside wall. Forty-seven degrees below zero.

We walked back to our new home. The dogs had quietened down, the saws were still, and we could hear the compacted snow crunch beneath our feet.

"It's a whole new start," Dad said, "for us and the road. They've got army engineers up here locating the road, service regiments building it in sections. They're bringing up some black troops, too, from the South — Alabama, Georgia, Louisiana. Those poor fellas don't know what they're in for. This cold can snap steel."

"Just how long's this road going to be, Dad?"

"They say about twelve hundred miles through Canada and a couple of hundred through Alaska. A real American–Canadian union."

"Like our family," I said.

"But *their* agreement to build the highway was all written out *before* they made a move," Mom said.

I ran ahead to let them work it out. I knew Mom was trying to deal with the changes that had come so quickly. She'd accepted Dad's need for isolation and for being his own boss, and seemed happy living on the trapline. But it was hard to figure out his sudden change of mind. Was it brought on by the arrival of his brother, by patriotism, or by the chance to make money? He was a hard person to figure out.

I headed toward my sectioned-off bedroom. I'd be sleeping on the top bunk, Jody on the bottom, unless it was too cold for her and she'd have to come in with one of us. I lay awake, burrowed beneath my goose-down comforter. The moon illuminated the buttons of frost on the nail heads around me. This place wasn't as nice as our cabin on the Tanana River, but it was home now. And soon it would be spring.

I could hear Dad tossing around in the top bunk across the room from me. "You awake, Jay?" he asked, in a whisper.

"Yeah."

"We're not going to have much time off for the next month or so. They're working round-the-clock shifts to bring wood in to the mill before breakup. The whole place will be a sea of mud when the snow goes. Think you're up to it?"

"Sure." Then I whispered back, "What's tailing, Dad?" But he had gone to sleep.

I turned my back to the wall, feeling the draft blowing in through the cracks in the boards. A wolf howled, then another. Our dogs started up, joining their wild brothers. I fell asleep, listening to their familiar lullaby.

8

Highway Horrors

My job was mill hand. I did whatever I was asked to do, so each day was different.

First thing in the morning I harnessed Satin and Silky. Then I hitched up a stoneboat and roped on two forty-five-gallon barrels to haul water for the camp and for the mill boilers. I drove them a half mile to the river, chopped a hole in the river ice, dipped in a pail, and filled the drums. Within an hour a coating of ice formed over my mukluks from water spilling on them. My feet kept warm enough, but I clunked like a knight in armour. My hands were a real problem. They got wet, and right away my fingers stiffened with cold.

After our noon dinner, I worked at the mill. I found out what tailing was: taking lumber off the carriage that carried logs through the saws. I also flipped logs down the rollway and sometimes canted behind Dad, taking slabs off. Driving the horses, I skidded logs in from the bush. I was getting pretty good with horses. I liked them, and they liked me.

Because my school texts had been destroyed in the fire, I got a short holiday from homework. But Mom wrote right away, and the new books came in by airplane. For the first time, I wished airplanes were banished from the North!

Whenever the men joked about Mr. Knapp hiring school kids, Mom would glare at them. They quickly shut up then, likely thinking of her great bread and cinnamon buns, pies, and cakes. And Muskwa's pink stew.

I sometimes fell asleep over my books, although I tried to concentrate. I didn't want failing grades to bring on another argument between Mom and Dad.

"You're working him too hard!" Mom said to Dad after I'd dozed off while reading a chapter in my geography text about wind patterns. Their sharp voices woke me, but I kept my eyes closed.

"He's making a man's wage, he's going to do a man's work! I'm not favouring him over the other men."

"Men!" Mom spat out the word. "He's a boy — a schoolboy! If he fails these courses, I'm sending him back to Fairbanks to board right now, never mind waiting until fall. I've got my own money now, and I can do it."

Dad stomped out, slamming the door. I really tried hard after that. For a while, anyway.

Mr. Knapp had three mills: this one at Charlie Lake, a small portable mill at the Sikanni Chief River 120 miles north toward Fort Nelson, and a third mill 350 miles north of that at the Liard River. Eventually, we'd be moving to these mills as the highway progressed.

Whenever Uncle Matthew flew to Fort St. John, he would come out to see us. This evening he had joined us for supper at the mess-hall table.

"Otto's offered me a partnership," Dad told Uncle Matthew.

"Good. I was hoping he would."

"You and the old man — both determined to get me into the lumber business!"

"Don't compare us, Jed. It's not fair. This is a special case, a war effort. You're not likely to get as rich here as if you'd taken over the Seattle operation."

"Rich! Hah! I don't know why I'm buying this pile of junk," Dad said, after a minute. "I'll be running the mill at the Liard — with a six-cylinder diesel Jimmy engine and a T120 Chrysler to drive the mill, both held together with wire. Only thing good about them is they're cheap to repair. About two hundred bucks will buy a new block."

"You're in the right place at the right time," Uncle Matthew said. "This is still a country where a man can get ahead by good luck and hard work. It's a start for Jay, too." He nodded his head toward me, struggling with a math lesson.

Dad snorted. "If he kept his nose out of books he might learn something. I got a contract to supply bridge materials at the Liard. Six-by-six timbers. Jay can come up, learn the business firsthand. We'll be logging with crosscut or Swede saws. Lots of good pine and spruce in that country."

"What about Lilly?" Uncle Matthew looked at Mom, who was cleaning the kitchen, laughing as she threatened to throw a pan full of soapy water at Muskwa. She'd got him about 100 percent cleaner than he was before, but when she'd caught him washing his socks in the dish pan she realized the job wasn't done yet. Jody was running around between the kitchen and the mess hall, a favourite with the men, who missed their own wives and kids.

"Lilly seems to have adjusted. Think I'll leave her and Jody here until I get set up at the Liard."

"And Jay?"

"Oh, Lilly will likely kick up a fuss when I try to take him north, but I'm going to need him there sooner or later."

"Good luck," Uncle Matthew said, giving me a wink.

I ducked my head down to my book. It was weird to hear myself being discussed, as if I had nothing to say about it at all. Only Uncle Matthew seemed to understand. I tried to figure out what I wanted, but there was so much going on.

"How much education do I need to get into flying school, Uncle Matt?" I asked, but Dad interrupted before he had a chance to answer.

"Maybe Jay can go with Otto to Fort Nelson for a while," Dad said. "The school of hard knocks never hurt anyone. Otto's not easy to get along with, but he knows his business."

"Don't be too hard on the boy," Uncle Matthew said. "He's had a lot to learn in a short time."

But Dad's mind wasn't on my problems. "We've got to start moving camp as soon as possible, before the Fort Nelson trail is two feet deep in muskeg. When it thaws, I'll be isolated for a while."

"Plenty of places I can land." Uncle Matthew looked over at me. "I can take you, your Mom, and Jody to see your Dad if you get lonely for him."

Dad scowled and busily stirred his coffee. "We don't get lonely when we've got jobs to do."

It was hard to figure him out. Was he afraid we wouldn't miss him? Was he nervous about us travelling in Uncle Matthew's airplane again? Or was he just being cantankerous? I concluded it was all three.

One day, when the weather had changed with lightning speed from snow to warm Chinook winds, a truck driver came into camp on his way back from hauling supplies up the highway. His three-ton Ford churned ruts into the road and splattered the trees on either side with mud. Mr. Knapp brought him into the cookshack for a meal.

"You've no idea what's going on up that road." The driver settled back with his second cup of coffee. "Bulldozers churning the road open before the muskeg thaws. Cat-trains of ten sleighs pulled by D-7 Caterpillars inching along behind the dozers."

What I wouldn't give to be there! As the driver described conditions along the road, I pictured barges on the half-frozen river taking supplies and equipment up to the landing — graders, portable sawmills, blacksmith's forges, fuel, food.

"But none of those Southern boys knows how to drive on snow and ice," the driver said.

I imagined coming up over a rise and seeing a string of army trucks slithering around on the hill, crashing into one another.

"The army's issued orders that convoys must stay together. One starts slipping, where's the next guy going to go?" He banged his fist on the table, making the cups jump. "Men are being injured or killed every week on this confounded road."

I saw bodies wrapped in canvas being thrown onto trucks, taken to the M.O. — Medical Officer — for death certificates. Then the trucks getting stuck.

"It's a real mess, I'll tell you," the driver said.

I didn't know whether to believe him or not, but nobody gave me a sly wink.

"Just this morning at Blueberry Mountain I saw a convoy of trucks . . ."

I could see three of them, right over the bank. A group of black army men standing around, freezing in improper footgear, trying to eat off tin plates. They were trying to break off a chunk of food, but it was frozen into a solid lump.

The driver snorted in disgust and held his coffee cup out for another refill.

"Those poor outsiders must think hell's full of ice, not fire," Dad commented.

"Yep, everywhere you go, you hear stories," the driver went on. "The men are getting sick — flu, colds, first one then another, until they're all coughing, sneezing, energy gone. Back in February, early March, crews were in tents strung along the road. Bush, snow, forty, sixty below. Tents! One guy brings in a bottle. 'What's this?' 'Overproof rum, pal. Here, have a snort! It'll fix you up.' 'Well, it's slushy, but that's okay.' They each have a long drink, him and his mate." He paused dramatically, looking around the room. "Both those fellows were dead by morning."

I held my breath. Surely someone would say this was a lie!

"Froze them up inside." Dad said, nodding his head. "The liquor would've been the same temperature as the air."

The men continued eating. The room was quiet now, the only sounds being Muskwa and Mom in the kitchen and the crackle of the fire in the big heater. "There's a war going on overseas," the driver said, "but the war here with nature is just as deadly. Building this *top-secret* road to nowhere."

They talked on and I listened, my open schoolbooks giving me an excuse to hang around.

". . . protection of Alaska is of the greatest importance to the security of the U.S. Over ten thousand army men working here, building this big secret . . ."

". . . civilian vehicles are being stopped at Mile 101. Nobody can mention the highway in their letters home, but you pick up the paper — everything from the San Francisco *Chronicle* to the Calgary *Herald* — and there it is, black and white, the whole story. But if a soldier sends a clipping to his mom in Omaha, it's taken out by the censors."

"Letters aren't the only thing the government's burning. Machinery breaks down, it's pushed into the ditch and set afire."

"Why?"

"Costs too much to repair. How they going to fix carburettors and generators in sixty-below weather? Thing that gets me, we can't take any of this abandoned stuff — against customs regulations! So we watch machinery, food, clothing, furniture being bulldozed into useless dump piles, doused with gas, lit on fire, flames to the sky. It would make a preacher swear!"

"Big secret — shared by ten thousand, and that's only the army people."

"Then there's people like us, running sawmills," I said. The men turned toward me and stared, as if seeing me for the first time. There was a moment's silence, then their conversation resumed.

"And surveying, chopping three to four miles of road a day, twenty-four-hour shifts. Trucking, freighting, packing with horses," Dad said. "I've met Indian and white trappers, miners, Cat-skinners, loggers and rivermen working this project. Knowledgeable people."

"But some who couldn't find their way out of a red willow patch are also being hired as experts, simply because they lived here," the driver said. "Now *they're* directing where the road should go. Road locators are getting their heels nipped off by the bulldozers. Machinery breaks down, they push it over to the side of the trail. But leave a truck for ten minutes and it's stripped of every usable part!"

Dad agreed with the trucker. "This whole project is a show of power, wealth, and waste. Both material and human!"

The men got up to go back to work.

Otto Knapp pushed in his chair with a loud scrape. "If this road ever leads to Alaska, it'll be a miracle."

I turned back to my lesson, but the numbers swam in front of my eyes. I was living in the middle of the most exciting project in the country — fighting the war on the homefront — but here I was, having to study math and slog around all day in ice-covered mukluks, working as a mill slave. Learning to be a man, I guess.

9

Bugs in the River

Just after daybreak one morning I drove Satin and Silky
to the river for water as usual. The stoneboat tipped and
lurched on the muddy trail. I knew that half the water
would slop out on the way back and I'd have to double
my trips. When I got to the river I noticed that the ice
was ready to go out. I tested it with a pole. It wasn't bad
along the edges but not safe for the horses, so I took my
axe and went to look for a new chopping hole up ahead.

Then out of the corner of my eye I caught a movement
in the middle of the river, where a small rock island split
the flow. In the bush anything out of the ordinary — a
movement, a colour, a sign in the snow — is worth
checking. I squinted against the bright sunshine glint-
ing off the ice.

A man wearing a red plaid Mackinaw jacket was
trying to cross to my side. In his hand he carried a large
valise. He'd be crazy to try! I waved and called out to get

his attention. "No! Ice no good!" but he must not have heard me because he started anyway, zigzagging around broken shards of ice, jumping from one chunk to another. Dark water slopped over onto the ice chunks, making them slippery and dangerous. The breaking 'bergs groaned and heaved like bears coming out of hibernation. But the ice was deceptive — what seemed to be ice might actually be frozen foam, which would hold no weight.

"Stop! Go back!" I yelled.

This time he must have heard me because he turned back.

I began to chop a hole into the soft ice so I could start filling my pails. When I looked up again all I saw was the valise.

I tore off the iced rope securing the barrels to the stoneboat and looped it around my arm. Then I crawled out onto the groaning mass of broken ice toward where the valise lay.

Where was he? Then I saw two dark spots — gloved hands clinging to a shelf of ice. But that was all.

Like a crab, I dragged myself closer until I could see the ghostly outline of his body beneath the ice. If the cold hadn't killed him, he would be able to breathe air locked between the water and the ice.

I grabbed his hands and pulled, but the river current was stronger than me and pulled him back. I looped the lariat around the man's wrist and pulled again. But it was no use. I slid around like a seal on the water-slicked ice.

I edged back to shore, trying not to hear the moans of the rotting ice. The ice shelf he'd been clinging to broke away, but fortunately the current brought him nearer to shore. I quickly unhitched Silky from the stoneboat and led her, stamping and nervous, to the river's edge. Again I slithered out onto the mass of broken ice and half-frozen water. I managed to grab the rope around his wrist and edged back. I scrambled up the gravelled bank and tied the rope to the harness traces. "Giddap, Silky! Pull, girl!"

The man's body emerged from the water, bumping over a ridge. I half dragged, half carried him to the stoneboat, threw off the barrels, and laid him on his stomach across the icy platform of the stoneboat. Then I hitched up Silky and headed for home.

I ran behind the stoneboat, not wanting to ride with the man in case he was dead. His face and ears were blue, eyes open, and water ran from unmoving lips. I started yelling even before reaching camp. "Help! I found a man! Frozen! Help!"

Men came running and carried the body into the cookshack. Muskwa turned him onto his back and straddled his hips. With one hand over the other, he pressed the heel of his bottom hand into the man's abdomen. Two, three quick upward thrusts. Water gushed out the man's mouth and he began to cough and gasp for air.

Mom handed me a steaming cup of hot chocolate as I stood shivering and watching my dead man come to life. His eyes seemed to focus. He looked around. My world stopped spinning.

"You're okay, Son. You'll be fine," Muskwa said.

"Where am I?"

"At a camp. That boy there saved your hide! You were nearly a goner."

He looked about eighteen years old, string-bean thin. His shirt and pants were about three inches too short. The man's blue eyes turned toward me. "Thanks," he whispered.

"What's your name, boy?" Muskwa asked.

The man said something that sounded like "Bugs," then closed his eyes.

"That's right. You have a good sleep now, Bugs."

Muskwa untied the man's boots and slipped them off his feet. "City boots!" Muskwa said disgustedly. A quart of water poured from each one. He took Bugs's wet clothes off and wrapped him in blankets. "Doesn't look like he's had a square meal in weeks."

"We'll soon fix that," Mom said. She turned to me. "Now, let's get you home and out of those wet clothes."

Outside, Silky and Satin were waiting nervously, pawing at the ground. I went over and rubbed their noses. "Good horses!" One of the men took them away to give them some oats and a rest while I went to change my clothes.

Mom walked back to the shack with me. She stoked up the fire while I went behind my partition, pulled off my wet clothes, and put on warm long underwear and socks. Suddenly my body felt shaky, my limbs heavy, like I was going to faint. "I think I'll lie down for just a minute," I said, crawling up onto my bunk.

"That was a brave thing you did, Jay," she said.

"Silky did the pulling. I just gave the orders."

After I heard Mom leave, I lay listening to the fire in the stove. The walls crackled as the heat chased out the frost.

I must have dozed off because next thing I knew Mom and Dad were back in the cabin, having a real go-round. It was, as usual, about me.

"You're wrecking this kid's life! He's near exhaustion, working ten hours a day and then trying to study. And he could have drowned, pulling that man out of the river!"

"It's not me who's making him study, and it's not me who asked him to pull that monkey out of the river!"

"Don't call him a monkey. He's a young man who got into trouble. He doesn't know the country very well. But he's smart. I was talking to him, he worked in a bank. I think we could use him."

"What? A useless little city boy! You think we should hire him!"

Their voices carried on, up and down. I lay quiet, not wanting to get into the middle of it.

"I'm making a man out of that boy there," Dad said, likely indicating me. "If you want a kid who looks like a tap dancer and works in banks, start working on Jody. But Jay's soon going to be a man, and he's going to learn a man's trade. He'll be able to make a good living, running a sawmill for anyone, anywhere!"

"Your father tried to do that with you, and you ran away. Now you're shipping your own son to some godforsaken mill to study under a dog like Knapp. He's staying here! He needs his schooling. He needs me!"

"*I* need him right now. The *outfit* needs him. He can study at night."

I waited until they went outside, then got up.

In the evening, when I stopped in at the mess hall for supper, the river man was there. Mom had set a bowl of beef stew and dumplings in front of him and was now coming out of the kitchen with a plate of fried eggs and sausages.

"Hi, Bugs!" I said. "Do you remember me?"

"I sure do. I've got a lot to thank you for." He grinned, then looked puzzled. "But why is everyone calling me Bugs?"

"That's what you said!"

He laughed. "My name is Barry Nuggs. I was half frozen when I said it, and maybe it came out Bugs! Hey, you want to call me Bugs, I don't mind."

"Okay, Bugs," I said, piercing a steaming dumpling.

"Your mom sure is a fine person," Bugs said. "She thinks maybe I can get a job here. I've never worked in a sawmill, but I can learn."

"What did you do, before?"

Bugs's face turned red, and he concentrated on his supper, avoiding looking at me. "I'm a bank clerk."

"A what?"

"Ssshh! Don't let the men hear! I worked in a bank. In Edmonton. I heard about the highway and I wanted to see it."

"So how'd you get in the river?"

His face turned redder. "I was going up to one of the army camps. I heard they were hiring civilians to ride pack horses."

I burst out laughing. I couldn't help it. "Look, Bugs, come with me tomorrow morning when I get water. I'll tell you a few things about mills and the North. And I'll give you Lesson Number One right now: you don't *ride* pack horses!"

"And you don't cross rivers when the ice is going out," he said.

"Right. But you've done one smart thing. You've impressed Mom. If you've got her pushing for you, you'll likely be bossing a crew next week!"

Mom was a definite hit with the mill crew. She was pretty, pleasant, and her cooking was fabulous. The men called her "Ma'am." Muskwa was like a puppy around her. Everyone knew it was Mom who really ran the kitchen now, with Muskwa happy to follow her menu suggestions or ideas for little parties. Now the mens' birthdays were big deals.

At Easter, Uncle Matthew was flying a Catholic priest to two army camps and persuaded him to come and say Mass for the twenty people at our camp, too. The night before Easter, April 4, we had a crazy spring storm, with snowflakes the size of goose feathers, and we thought the priest wouldn't come. But just after supper Uncle Matthew drove into camp with Father Guichon in a sleigh he'd borrowed. Everyone, Catholic or not, gathered in the mess hall.

Mom, pumping furiously on her harmonium, played and sang "Ave Maria." When she sang "Holy Holy," first one man, then another joined in. The gas lamps shone on tear-stained faces, and our singing often halted as voices caught.

"Our music makes a brave protest against the storm that rages tonight," Father Guichon said, "as well as against the magnitude of the war raging overseas."

When the service was over, the priest joined in our celebrations. Muskwa got his fiddle, Mrs. Knapp her concertina, and two mill hands had harmonicas. When someone played the first bar others joined in, whether they were on key or not.

"I think you should go professional," Uncle Matthew said, clapping his hands to the fast beat of "Turkey in the Straw." "Call yourselves The Mill Band. Play for dances all over the country. I'll handle bookings!"

Uncle Matthew sang the loudest, but he was tone-deaf.

One of the men went up to him. "Aren't you Midnight Smith?" he asked.

"Well, yes, some do call me that."

"Hey, this guy's a hero!" the man said to us. "He's saved more people than — "

"Oh, cut it out!" Uncle Matthew laughed. "We're here to party."

From the back of the room, we heard the fast clomp of a two-step. The men parted to let the dancer through. Out came Bugs, in his plaid shirt, braces hitching up his pants just like a real logger. His feet, in heavy boots, flew about as he jigged to the music. Round and round he spun, his boots pounding a crazy tattoo on the board floor.

"More!" the men shouted.

Bugs stopped to mop his glistening face and untie his boots. Then, in his wool socks, he danced "The Sailor's Hornpipe."

At the end of the dance, he flung himself into a chair, exhausted. I went over and sat down beside him. "How'd you learn those dances?" I asked.

His red face became redder. "My mom and I lived over a dance school."

We watched the men jig around the room. There were only two women to dance with, Mom and Mrs. Knapp, who took turns dancing and making the music.

Sometimes we got in a circle, two-stepping and yelling "Hey!" and swinging each other around by the elbow like in a square dance. A couple of times Mom left the harmonium, and she and Dad whirled around on the rough plank floor. She was laughing, not caring that her hair came undone from its neat "victory roll" to fall around her neck. Dust rose as the floor bounced in rhythm to the pounding feet, the dancing becoming faster and wilder as song followed song. I picked Jody up in my arms, and she giggled as we twirled around.

When the sun rose, Muskwa went into the kitchen and cooked up ham and eggs, as exhaustion from the dancing and the smell of coffee and breakfast brought our party to a halt. We gathered again at the tables, realizing then that we'd never left the mess hall since last night's supper. Only Jody had gone to sleep.

Otto Knapp had lost one shift of work and hadn't said a word.

10

Heroes and Madmen

CANADA FIGHTING FOR ITS LIFE

If the enemy is not defeated on distant oceans and on other continents, then the final battles will be fought on the waters and soils of Canada and the United States, says Canadian Prime Minister Mackenzie King.

"I want you to go to the Sikanni Chief River," Dad said, the next day. "Otto has taken a portable mill there by Cat train. Learn everything he can teach you. He won't be an easy boss, but it'll be worth it to you in the long run."

"Why?"

"So you can *learn* something! You'll never make a living reading books. When you join me later at the Liard, you'll know enough so you can run the show if I have to leave."

There was nothing more I could say. I wanted to tell him I'd like to make my own decisions once in a while about where I went and what to do with my life. Also, in case he hadn't thought of it, it was the first time I'd ever left my family. But I didn't have time to utter a word.

"Better pack your clothes and bedroll," Dad said

curtly. "We're meeting Matt in Fort St. John. He's going to the Sikanni Chief with a load of cargo. You can fly up with him."

Wow! Another plane trip with Uncle Matt! I threw my clothes together, rolled my bedding around the lump, and tied it up with rope. I grabbed my gun and ammunition, and began to whistle as I headed out to the waiting wagon.

When I got to the wagon, I had even more to whistle about: Bugs was hoisting his valise onto the wagon box. "Hey, what's going on?"

He turned toward me, an ear-splitting grin on his face.

"Mr. Knapp has hired me for the Sikanni mill, too! I'm going to be a bull cook!"

"Hey, that's great!"

"Uh, what's a bull cook, Jay?"

I explained that he would be cleaning out bunk houses, sweeping up the cookshack, chopping kindling, doing almost everything to keep the camp in order.

"Oh, that's okay. I don't mind hard work." When he laughed his freckles seemed to scramble around his face. His hair stood up in front, like an exclamation point.

I laughed, too. Bugs was so thrilled at being in the North that he'd do anything to stay.

"Hey, we'll both work hard and try to get on Otto's good side," I said.

It would be fun to have a friend closer to my age along. There were so many things I wanted to ask him. What was it like to live in a city like Edmonton? Were there lots of nice girls there? Did he take them out dancing? Maybe, after he went back to the city, I could go visit him some time.

Mom hugged me. "Take care of yourself, Jay. And try to keep up your studies. Jody and I will join you soon."

Jody, imitating her, offered a sticky hug.

Dad drove us to Fort St. John by wagon, pulled by Satin and Silky. He held the reins to what I considered my team now.

"Otto will be doing the millwrighting — setting up, making sure the carriage track carrying the logs and the saw are in proper alignment," Dad said. "You'll be canting and tailing, and if he needs you to cook, you'll do that, too."

"I can cook!" Bugs said, but Dad ignored him.

"You two will do what you're told, and don't go getting any ideas."

"He said maybe I'd be running the Johnson bar to do the sawing, pushing logs through to make lumber," I said.

"He'll have to see if you're any good at it. You need a sharp eye to judge logs for different sizes of lumber. And a head for fractions to figure how much lumber you can get out of a log."

"Don't worry. I get good marks in math."

"You won't have time to do much math! I'll see what you've learned about real work when you come up to the Liard. I'm going there in a couple of weeks, and I'll send for you when the mill's set up."

"Will you be flying in?"

"Maybe."

"Bringing the dogs?"

"I sold three of them to that truck driver."

I swallowed hard. "Which ones?"

"Brutus, Bess, Shiloh. They aren't any use to us anymore."

"You mean . . . we're not going back to the trapline?"

"Not for a while."

"Not ever? We could build a new cabin somewhere else."

But he turned his head away as if he hadn't heard

me. I couldn't look at Bugs. I was ashamed he'd see
tears. It was the wind that caused them, but Bugs
wouldn't know that.

I looked over the backs of the two horses. Their strong
black haunches lifted and fell as they pulled us through
the muddy road. Had we been here only three weeks? It
seemed like three years.

When we got to Fort St. John, there were men and
horses and trucks everywhere. Dad was heading for the
foundry to pick up a bearing for the bulldozer. Bugs and
I jumped out of the wagon. "Meet you later at the hotel
cafe."

We walked up and down the muddy board sidewalks
of the main street, looking in store windows, watching
and listening to the strange assortment of people. Well-
dressed ladies and gentlemen. Ranchers. Indians and
trappers. Bushmen with slouch hats and overalls.

We met Uncle Matthew coming out of the barbershop.
"Just had my ears lowered," he said with a laugh. "Looks
like you two could use the same," and suddenly I found
myself sitting in the barber chair.

"Give him the works, Joe," Uncle Matthew ordered,
and I was caped and shorn.

"Next time you're in you'll be needing a shave," the
barber joked. "How about this renegade?" He indicated
Bugs.

"You look like new men," Uncle Matthew said a short
time later as he paid the barber.

I caught my reflection in the window. Hey!

We were walking down the street when the door of
the Fort Hotel beer parlour burst open and a fight
tumbled onto the sidewalk. A crowd of soldiers surged
out to watch. We wedged our way through to see what
was happening.

A burly military policeman was trying to pound his
opponent into the ground. The man underneath

whipped his leg up around the M.P.'s neck and flipped him off. He jumped to his feet.

"Dad!" I cried, and started forward, but Uncle Matthew grabbed my shoulders. I turned to a man standing beside me. "What's the fight about?"

"That army cop won't let the black soldiers drink in the beer parlour. Thinks he's still in the South." He turned his attention back to the fight.

"Get 'im, Dad!" I yelled, then wished I hadn't said "Dad." It might throw off his concentration, knowing his kid was watching. "Get 'im, Jed!" I yelled, feeling funny calling my dad by his first name.

"Ya got 'em where you want 'im now, Mr. Smith!" Bugs yelled, waving his fist.

"Your dad's got guts," Uncle Matthew said.

The fight ended with both men looking torn, bedraggled, and completely winded, but the winner was obviously Dad. He hadn't beaten the other guy, he'd just run him into the ground, like a wolf will run a moose until it gives up from sheer exhaustion. Dad wiped blood from his lip and turned to his opponent, who was sitting on the sidewalk, his uniform jacket torn at one shoulder. Dad was panting.

"Treat your men like men, understand?"

A cheer went up from the crowd. I went to Dad and held out my hand. "So long," I said. He shook my hand and smiled crookedly at Bugs and me with swelling lips. And that's how we said good- bye.

Before we headed north, Uncle Matthew flew forty-five miles south toward Dawson Creek, Mile Zero on the highway, to show us where the road started. "Dawson Creek used to have a population of six hundred before the highway began," Uncle Matthew said. "Now it's five thousand and growing." Below me I could see long rows of army tents spread over the fields.

We flew back over the Peace River, then over our mill

site at Charlie Lake. I thought of my family, the horses, and my dogs — or dog now — below, tinier than the dollhouse and little people that Dad had made for Jody.

"I have to drop some cargo at Fort Nelson," Uncle Matthew said. "I'll take you there first. You should see the place."

"Great!" I hollered over the sound of the engine.

"Think you're going to like being on your own?"

"You bet!"

"The men might be hard on you. You're young. And Bugs is pretty green. And your dad's part owner. You'll be the boss's kid."

I shrugged.

"Otto can be a bear cat." He looked over at me. "Can you handle him?"

"Sure."

I'll have to, I thought. He can't be any tougher than my father.

Foggy grey ghosts wafted between the airplane and the ground, over the Beatton River. As we flew north, we could see the equipment site at the Sikanni Chief River.

"It took the Cat-trains three days to get down the three-mile Sikanni hill," Uncle Matthew said. "They had to bulldoze, blast, and build bridges. One sleigh at a time, inching along, the rest waiting, chained to trees. The Indians thought they were mad. Probably right."

When we reached Fort Nelson, my ears were buzzing so much I could hardly hear for a few minutes. A doctor was waiting for the first pilot to come in to make an emergency flight. An Indian boy up near Fort Liard was having an appendicitis attack. He needed to get the kid back to the army medical centre at Mile 8 in Fort Nelson for treatment.

Uncle Matthew handed me a twenty-dollar bill. "Here, get a couple of rooms at the hotel. I'll see you when I see you." He looked up at the sky. Tall black clouds were forming. "It's going to be another of those seat-of-the-pants trips."

We watched the plane until it was out of sight, then hitched a ride in an army vehicle to town. There was no downtown here.

Fort Nelson had been built as a trading centre where the Prophet, Muskwa, and Sikanni Chief joined and formed the Fort Nelson River, but now it was busy with people working on the highway, army personnel, and civilians.

The army guy let us off at the only "hotel" in town, an army shack — the British Yukon Navigation Staging Post — which he called "the B.Y.N." I went inside and asked a man sweeping the floor if we could get rooms. I didn't know how far my twenty dollars would go, but the rooms were only two dollars each. I was rich! Bugs and I put our gear in our rooms and went off to explore.

In the front part, which was more an entry way than a lobby, with a couple of chairs along one side, I noticed a girl about my age and a younger boy looking at everyone who came in.

We walked out to the street and watched the action for a while. Men in U.S. Army uniforms were everywhere. Unlike Fort St. John, where many Indians and white trappers came to town to spend their fur money, there were very few here, and those I saw seemed to be doing their business and not hanging around. The army guy had told us that the Indians lived mostly on the other side of the Nelson River and seldom came to town. One trapper approached leading two beautiful sleigh dogs. When I stopped to admire them, he told me they were a cross between Russian wolfhound and Husky. I said our team were Great Dane and wolf cross. Suddenly I wondered if I'd ever run behind a dog team again.

The wind was blowing like crazy so we went back to

the hotel. I stopped to read the notices tacked to the wall outside.

PRIVATE ALBERT PETERSEN, A.W.O.L.
SINCE MARCH 3, 1942.

And, more seriously:

$1,000 WILL BE PAID TO ANYONE
KNOWING THE WHEREABOUTS OF
LIEUTENANT JACOB FARRELL WHO
DISAPPEARED APRIL 1, 1942, WHILE
FLYING A P-40 FROM LOS ANGELES TO
LADD FIELD. LAST KNOWN
COMMUNICATION BETWEEN FORT NELSON
AND WATSON LAKE.

The girl and boy were still sitting in the entry way. Bugs sat down beside the boy.

"You live here?" he asked him.

"No. Our father is picking us up. He's got business in the city."

"Sshhh." The girl elbowed her brother.

"And I'm hungry," he said. I could see dried tear stains on his face. "We had a sandwich this morning — "

"Teddy, don't tell people our business." The girl's voice quavered a bit, and I could see she was trying to act braver than she felt. I sat down beside her.

"My name is Jay Smith, and this is Bugs, er, Barry. We're on our way to the Sikanni Chief River to run a sawmill. We're waiting for my uncle. He's a pilot and he had to go on a mercy flight."

"A pilot? Holy cow!" said the boy.

"Why don't you come and have something to eat with us? We don't know anybody here," Bugs said.

"We can't," said the girl. "We have to watch for father."

Her hand kept going to her suitcase, as if to make sure it was there.

"You'd like some supper, wouldn't you?" I said to the boy. "By the way, what's your name?

"Teddy Braden. I'm five. That's my sister Loretta. She's fourteen-and-a-half. And we haven't any money!"

"Well, I do, and I'm treating you," I said. "Now come on. I'm hungry."

Teddy was out of his chair, his little suitcase in his hand, before we could say another word. Bugs took his other hand and headed out the door. I waited for Loretta. She looked up at me, her blue eyes brimming with tears. I sat down beside her and, I don't know why, held out my arms. She suddenly burst into sobs. It was strange feeling her head on my shoulder, the wetness of her tears against my neck.

"There, there," I said, remembering Mrs. Mackenzie's soothing words to Mom. I patted her shoulder. "You'll be fine. We'll go and get something to eat, and before you know it, your father will be here."

Somehow, in my first hour in Fort Nelson, I had got to know the most beautiful girl I'd ever met. The *only* one my age I'd seen since school in Fairbanks — and I was just a kid then.

11

Romance at the B.Y.N.

U.S. PLANES BOMB FOUR JAPANESE CITIES

Japan announced today that allied planes,
taking the war to Japan for the first time, had
bombed Tokyo, Yokohama, Kobe and Nagoya.

I asked the man who'd given us our rooms where we
could go for supper. There was no restaurant in the
hotel, but he told me about a place called the Nite Owl
Cafe that was part of a store. You paid seventy-five cents
and got your meal from a big table at the back. No one
asked us what business we had in Fort Nelson. That's
the way people were in the North: nobody asked what
you were up to, where you were from, or where you were
going. If you volunteered the information, okay, but they
didn't dig it out of you.

Teddy volunteered everything.

"Our mom's dead," he said as he mixed his turkey and
gravy with a mound of mashed potatoes. "I don't know
what father's going to do with us. We haven't seen him
for a long time. He works at night. With cards."

"Cards?" Bugs was suddenly interested. "I play
cards!"

"Ssshhh!" Loretta jabbed Teddy in the ribs to shut him up. This was getting interesting.

"Anyway, we're not staying in this little town," Teddy said proudly. "We're going to the city where father has his business. It's called Weasel City."

Loretta jabbed him so hard I thought he'd spill his dinner.

"Weasel City," I said. "That sounds like a right fancy place." I avoided Bugs's eyes so we wouldn't burst out laughing.

Loretta stood up. Her face was red with anger, her eyes sparking.

"I think *you* are a weasel, Jay Smith," she hissed. "You start off being nice, but you're really making fun of us. There *is* a place called Weasel City, and I'll bet it's a sight better than that rotten old sawmill at the Sikanni Chief where you're going!"

I tried to wipe the smile off my face. "I'm sorry," I said. Loretta sat down again and finished her dinner. With two pieces of pie. By then we were laughing and talking as if we'd known each other forever.

We walked back to the hotel. Loretta and I walked slowly, letting Teddy and Bugs go on ahead.

"I guess you've lived in lots of places," Loretta said. "You must have friends everywhere."

"For the last three years we lived on a trapline. I didn't have a chance to meet anyone my age. I take school by correspondence."

"Do you like writing letters?"

"I've never had anyone to write to.

"Would you like a pen pal?"

"Like who?"

She blushed. "Me, maybe."

"I guess that would be all right."

"What's your address?"

I stopped. "I guess General Delivery, Fort St. John.

But, maybe I won't be back there. After the Sikanni, I'm going up to the Liard. And then . . . I don't know."

She laughed. "You write me first, then, okay? General Delivery, Weasel City, B.C. Father has a business there. Everyone will know us."

I couldn't help laughing, thinking of this pretty girl living in a place called that. I pretended I was chuckling at something Teddy was doing so she wouldn't get mad again. Hey, maybe I was learning how to act around girls!

Already the wind seemed warmer. Soon the snow would be melting, even in the shady places, and we'd smell new grass and leaf buds. Although it wasn't dark yet, it was late. The daylight hours of summer were just beginning. By the end of June I'd be able to read until ten o'clock without lighting a lamp.

When we got back to the B.Y.N., the man said their father hadn't shown up.

"Loretta and Teddy can wait for their father in my room," I told the man. "Please tell him when he comes."

Loretta looked grateful. It felt good helping them out.

"Well, I'm hitting the sack," Bugs said. "Good night."

Loretta, Teddy, and I went into my room and sat down on the bed. Teddy's eyes began to droop. In a few minutes he was stretched out fast asleep. Loretta took off his shoes and put them carefully by the door, then covered him with her coat.

We glanced at each other, suddenly shy as we realized we were alone. I looked at her face in the shady light. Her skin looked so soft; I wanted to touch it. Blonde curls fell onto her neck and down her back. Her eyes were as blue as the forget-me-nots Mom grew — used to grow — in our garden back at the Tanana River.

"I don't really have a home anymore," I said suddenly.

She looked at me, and I knew she understood. I reached over and touched her hand. She didn't pull back.

Oh gosh, now what? I wished I'd had time to ask Bugs about these kinds of situations. I could hear my heart pounding. She moved her hand back a bit. I had to do something. I pulled her hand toward me, and we laughed. I kept pulling until her face wasn't two inches from mine. Then I kissed her.

After a moment she moved back and sat on the edge of the bed. "We'd better not," she said.

I barely heard her over the roar in my ears. My hand touched her shoulder, her hair.

"This has to last a long time," I said, leaning toward her. Her arms went up, hesitantly, around my neck. I could feel her fingers touch the back of my head, then she got a better grip and held on tight. I shivered.

"Jay?"

"Yeah?"

"We'll always be friends, won't we?"

"Sure."

"You'll write to me?"

"Yeah. I'd like to have you for a friend."

There was a knock at the door. We flew apart, Loretta almost landing on Teddy. As I went to answer it I could hear the deep wheezes of an angry man.

A bearded giant pushed past me. "Loretta! Teddy!"

Loretta looked startled, not ready to have our visit come to such a sudden end. Teddy's eyes opened wide. The man roughly pulled him into a sitting position.

"I got held up. Big contract," the man said. "We gotta get outa here, right now!"

"But father." Loretta finally found her voice. "It's late! Can't we stay?"

"Right now, I say," her father answered. Then he saw me. "Who're you?"

"Jay Smith."

"Smith! Everyone around here's a Smith. No pasts.

No pedigrees." He laughed, showing big horsey teeth, then sobered. "Smith? That for real?"

He had broken the Northern code.

"Where you from?" he persisted.

I looked him in the eye. "The Tanana River area, but my dad mined out of Eagle for a while."

He jumped toward me. "Jed Smith? You kin to Jedediah Smith?"

"Could be."

"He your old man?"

"Maybe."

Loretta was looking from her father to me, wondering what the problem was. Teddy was rubbing his eyes, too tired to care.

"You don't tell your daddy nothin'," he said, leaning so close I could feel his hot breath. "You don't tell him you ever laid eyes on William J. Braden."

Then it hit me. I was staring straight into the eyes of the shrew.

"I'm beholden to you for helping out my kids, but we don't want no truck with any of you."

He picked up Teddy and threw him over his shoulder like a sack of potatoes. "Come on, Loretta!" She picked up their baggage and grabbed Teddy's shoes. At the door, she turned and waved her fingers at me.

"Write!" she mouthed.

I nodded, missing her already. There was so much more I'd wanted to say. I wondered what kind of home Loretta and Teddy would have in Weasel City. What would happen to them if someone ran them out?

Uncle Matthew came in late in the night. He was dead tired. "I've been to hell and back, Jay," he said, "but we saved the kid. Now I need some shut-eye."

He lay down and was soon asleep.

I tried to go back to sleep, but it was impossible. I took my math text out of my knapsack, went to the lobby, and tried to study, but I couldn't concentrate. I could hear drunken soldiers fighting outside on the street.

When I returned to the room, Uncle Matthew was having a nightmare. I almost woke him, but he settled down again. At times his face resembled Dad's, at times I thought he looked a lot like me. I felt proud that he was a part of us.

Would I ever see Loretta again? I tried to imagine what really happened between our fathers. And what William J. Braden would be doing for a living in Weasel City. I had an idea, and it wasn't pretty.

12

Midnight Smith and Me

JAPANESE THRUST AT ALEUTIANS
LIKELY MOVE

Japan is very likely to reply to the recent
bombing raids on four of her big cities with an
attack on the Aleutian Islands, those stepping
stones which extend 1,200 miles west of Alaska,
and provide Canada and the U.S. with their
closest bases to the Japanese homeland.

Uncle Matthew slept until noon the next day. Bugs and
I wandered around a bit, but there wasn't much to do
and the streets were like rutted trails. All the action in
the area went on at the army camp a couple of miles
away. Later that evening, we all went over to the Nite
Owl Cafe for a meal. As we ate, people kept coming over
to talk.

"Some spring this is! Three inches of snow just fell in
Whitehorse. Then we get suicide weather."

"Midnight, that was a crazy thing to do, even for you!"
a pilot said, slapping him on the back. "Those cumulo-
nimbus zapping with lightning! Remember, there's old

pilots and bold pilots but no old bold pilots!" He laughed and walked away.

Uncle Matthew bent his head down and concentrated on eating.

"Hey, I just saw the doc!" another man called. "Says any more of those kind of flights, he's retirin'. Gonna get him a nice little practice in some city where he don't have to risk *his* life for every one he saves!"

"Wow! I wish I'd been with you!"

"You're a hero!" Bugs said.

Uncle Matthew gave him a stern look. "It has nothing to do with being a hero, Bugs. It was just dumb luck. Some day thousands of people will drive the Alcan. Road signs telling them where they are. But up in the sky, there's nothing except poor maps and hopefully a good memory."

Two other pilots came in, got plates, and sat down beside us. Uncle Matthew introduced them as Cannonball Skelton and Bud Bezanson.

"Like to know how your Uncle Midnight got his nickname?" asked Bud.

"Yeah — 'cause he can see in the dark."

"Sure, but he cheats! Hey, Midnight! You still carry burlap sacks to throw out to get your bearings?" Cannonball said. He turned to me. "Sometimes you can't tell what's what, when sky and snow and ice are blurred in whiteouts. Your uncle throws sacks out of the plane."

"How come?"

"So he can tell where the ground is! You ever get a patent on that idea?"

Uncle Matthew just laughed.

"My uncle is teaching me to fly," I said, proudly.

"Oh, yeah? He send you for a bucket of prop wash yet?"

"Or mag drops?"

"Huh?"

The pilots laughed. "Rookie assignments," Bud said solemnly. "You get 'em everywhere when there are new men on the job."

"Oh."

"Your uncle saved my life once," Bud said. "Crashed my Fokker in the Glacier Mountain range. Everyone gave up on me. But not Midnight Smith! Kept coming back till he found me — twenty days! Saw the message I'd scratched on the clear ice with an axe blade. Man, I was a walking skeleton!"

"How was this trip?" Cannonball asked.

Uncle Matthew shrugged. "Went through a lightning storm. I just turned all the electricity off — lights, radio."

"If he happened to hit some lightning, it could blow his electrical circuit," Cannonball said to me. "So he just sat back and enjoyed the ride! Read a newspaper lit up by the sheet lightning. Midnight's got night-eyes anyway! Lightning changes everything, though."

"You pilots know where all the mountains, lakes, and stuff are, don't you?" I asked.

The pilots laughed, and I felt foolish.

"Sure you know where you are — but you can't pick your mountain. One is just as hard as another. Same as the ground, if you hit it at the wrong angle."

Then Uncle Matthew became serious.

"When the clouds roll in like linebackers — you play football, Jay? No, I guess not in the bush — anyway, these clouds were as high and far as I could see. Forty-five minutes worth of gas left. No turning back with Doc and the kid. Lightning stabbing like a bunch of pitchforks."

"Oh yes!" Bud said. "Music to our ears! Rain pounding. Engine banging its brains out. Plane rocking and plunging."

Uncle Matthew gave a shrug and a grin. "It was touch

and go this time, but I followed the Liard River down, then the Nelson River up to Fort Nelson. If the weather got too bad, I knew I had an airport under me — on the river. About the time I'd decided to camp — running low on fuel — the weather cleared. I could see the lights of the army camp near Fort Nelson."

"Oh, man!"

Bud leaned toward me. "You ever see your uncle take off from a short runway?" I shook my head. "Well, one time he landed in a little open area behind the hospital in Fairbanks. Had a patient. Time to go, doesn't think there's room for takeoff. So he ties a rope to a tree, the other end to the tail. Gives an axe to a guy standing there. Says, 'When this buggy starts lifting, you chop!' Then he redlines it, throttle through the fire wall. The man hauls back on that axe, his back to the prop blast, and cuts 'er clean through. Midnight roars off in that old Norseman with his wheels smackin' the trees."

"That's amazing!" I turned to Uncle Matthew. "Is that true?"

He laughed. "It might work," he said dryly. "But we do take too many risks. Plane loaded heavy in the tail, can't get the tail up. It won't take off. The back end stays on the ground, your front end wants to fly. And you just flip over, butt over apple cart."

"The organized crashes we can handle," Cannonball said. "It's the unorganized ones that kill us."

"Any fool can fly a plane," Uncle Matthew laughed, "but it takes a darn good pilot to crash 'em properly!"

Everyone laughed. It felt great to be part of the group.

"Why do you fly?" Bugs asked my uncle. "Risk your life taking chances?"

"Oh, I guess I'm a lot like Jay's dad — have to challenge everything. I've done some real stupid things — "

"Like what?"

The pilots leaned back, grinning.

"I shouldn't be telling you," Uncle Matthew said. "But, back in Washington, I flew under bridges once or twice. But hey, the bridges down there are a lot bigger than these little log trestles you see here! They're long and sleek and made of steel that lasts a lifetime."

"Yeah, like you'll see when you come to Edmonton!" Bugs said, to me. I ignored him, thinking he was trying to make me feel like a hick.

"You're either a flyer or you're not," Uncle Matthew said. He got up. "Come on, boys, let's put Nellie to bed."

We said good night to Bud and Cannonball and went down to the river to check the plane. Uncle Matthew looked up at the clear sky and the moon over the water. "So beautiful and calm one moment," he said. "God's storehouse of action the next."

"Sometimes it's like that down here," I said. "We have fires, blizzards. A hundred rivers in June, one river blocked with sandbars in September."

"You ever been up on the Liard, Jay?"

"Not yet."

"Well, that's one beauty of a river — from the air. But when you're navigating it by boat, you come across places like Hell's Gate, Devil's Portage, Whirlpool Canyon, Rapids of the Drowned. Gives you a strong message, doesn't it? Yet men challenge it every year."

"Maybe humans weren't meant to live here. Maybe we're just wrecking it all."

Uncle Matthew sat down on a log. Bugs went down to the river's edge, I guess sensing that I wanted to be alone with my uncle. We didn't say anything for a while, just looked around at the darkening shadows of the forest. The wind picked up a bit and stirred last year's dried grasses along the river bank. Twigs, still brittle from the winter's frost, clicked like crickets.

"Where is Weasel City?" I asked.

"Oh, a little bit north and west of New York City." he said solemnly.

"Come on! I'm serious. I met this girl, and she was moving there."

"You got a girlfriend? Who?"

"No, not a girlfriend. Just a girl I met. Loretta."

"Loretta who?"

"Braden."

Uncle Matthew was silent a moment. "One of Bean Trap Braden's kids?"

"No. He said his name is William J. Braden."

"It's got to be the same guy. He's bad news."

"Why do they call him Bean Trap?"

"It's slang for swindler. A guy who traps other men's beans, or money. Usually in rigged card games, that kind of thing. There's always a Bean Trap where there's money, and this highway's bringing them all in."

"What would he be doing here?"

"Oh, skimming off the army men. Ten thousand pay cheques would be too hard to resist."

"So where's Weasel City?"

"It's a small settlement of trappers' cabins out on the Muskwa River near Kledo Creek. Maybe Braden is running some kind of gambling operation out there to cheat the trappers out of their fur money. But I'd say he's likely using it for a base while he gets word to the highway crews. Civilians can't just walk into the army camps, you know."

"How would I get there?"

"Where? Braden's?"

"Just to Weasel City."

"Only by boat or airplane. Sorry . . . no dice."

"How come he knows Dad?" I asked.

But Uncle Matthew wouldn't answer.

"Come on. I have a right to know!"

"Ask Jed," he said sharply and stood up.

"I did. He just said he got rid of a shrew."

"All right. The boys at Eagle filled me in on the details. Your father burned down Braden's place. Bean Trap was running a crooked card game. He gypped the gold miners. Some of them worked for your dad. Their wives and kids were going to have a tough winter. They even came and asked Jed if he could do anything.

"Jed went over and told Braden to get out of town. As you can imagine, Braden told him to mind his own business. Jed gave him fair warning. Then . . . he torched his gambling house."

"No kidding!"

"Your Dad was charged with arson by the police. He went to jail for a couple of years. You'd be too young to know."

"I remember it. Mom and I moved to Grandma and Grandpa's in Dawson City for a while."

"No one was hurt in the fire. He'd made sure there wasn't anybody around. But it's against the law to burn someone's dwelling."

"So Braden was the crook, but Dad paid for it."

"Well, it made your dad pretty bitter. That's why he liked the isolation of the trapline. He'd have stayed there, if it wasn't for me."

"Maybe that's why he's so cranky sometimes. He doesn't want anything to do with people — "

"Your running into Loretta Braden might cause some problems. I don't think you should get too involved."

"But she had nothing to do with it! And neither did I."

"No, but Bean Trap's a mean snake. If you keep contact with Loretta and Bean Trap finds out where Jed is, sooner or later there could be trouble. He's basically a coward, but if he feels threatened, he might do something stupid."

"Like burning a cabin?"

"No, I don't think he'd do that. But there's more than one way to get back at someone if you're sore enough. Just keep out of his way. That's all."

"Maybe Bean Trap should be the one worrying! I'll bet he's got another gambling place in Weasel City."

"Likely. But he won't be there long. The police will run him out."

"My dad's hard to figure out, sometimes," I said. "In Eagle he got rid of Braden. In Fort St. John he stuck up for those black men. Boy, I never realized — "

"He's strong-willed, that's for sure," Uncle Matthew said. He looked at me and laughed. "Some might even call him bull-headed. But he gets things done. He's well-thought-of by the miners at Eagle, I can tell you that."

Bugs wandered back from the river bank clutching a twisted piece of driftwood. "I'm going to polish this — it will be my good luck club," he said.

"I guess it will do till Jay shows you how to handle a gun and shoot straight!" Uncle Matthew laughed.

"Oh, I'd *never* hold a gun, Mr. Smith," Bugs said. "I couldn't ever kill a living thing."

Oh gosh, I thought. What are you doing up here? Flashes of our life on the trapline came back. Hunting the winter's meat, trapping and pelting animals for money so we could live. I was suddenly sad, and I didn't know why.

We started walking back to the B.Y.N.

"You know, Uncle Matt, when you first met me I was running dogs. Then I had the horses. At the Sikanni Chief, I'll be operating a mill and driving a Cat. Dad's making me learn, and that's okay. I'll do it. But I'm not going back to the trapline. I know now what I really want to be."

"What's that?"

"A pilot. Like you."

"You're crazy. Weren't you listening today?"

"I'm going to fly all over the North — up to the Arctic Circle, over the tundra, through mountain passes, everywhere. I'll even fly over the Valley of Lost Planes."

His eyes bored into mine.

"Where is this crazy valley?" Bugs asked.

"You don't want to know."

"Yes, I do! Tell me," I said.

Uncle Matthew stopped and pulled a piece of paper out of his jacket pocket, a fuel bill or something, and drew a map. "Here," he said. "Now you know what place to avoid."

"When I'm a flier, I'll go everywhere," I said as I folded the map and tucked it inside my pocket. "Just like you. I won't be scared of anything."

"You're crazy."

"So are you."

"You both are," said Bugs.

An owl swooped down, so close that I could hear the beat of its wings. It spooked me.

13

Sikanni Chief

GREAT PACIFIC BATTLE RAGING

Fate of Australia in Balance

The next morning after we refuelled, we loaded up and got ready for takeoff. Uncle Matthew taxied to the centre of the river, and turned upstream.

"Show me how you get a plane up!"

"Water rudders up, at the same time bring the control column right back and ease on full throttle. Let it climb up on the step of the pontoon. Let off on the control column a little bit when you feel you're planing. Then, you're in the air!"

The pontoons bucked against the waves, faster and faster, skimming the top of the water, practically shaking my teeth out of my head.

"I hope those ropes hold the cargo!" he shouted over the roar of the engine. "We don't want to be wearing it on our heads."

He climbed through wispy clouds, veered to miss a flock of Canada geese heading north, and levelled out at six thousand feet.

"Want to take over for a while?"

"What? Me?"

"See anybody else in here?"

I settled behind the controls.

"Hold it lightly," Uncle Matthew said. "Don't grab. The airplane will fly all by itself. You just sort of guide it."

"Okay, I remember: keep the wings level by turning the control column. Keep the nose on the horizon by pulling back or pushing forward."

"But gently! You'll have us headed for the boonies!"

I looked over to see him grinning at me. Gee, I felt good.

Too soon Uncle Matthew indicated the Sikanni camp below us and motioned for me to let go of the column so he could take over.

"Thanks, Jay. You're not too bad a pilot."

I looked back at Bugs. His face was paper white, making his freckles appear even darker.

"Hey, it's all right! I did this before!" I yelled back.

He nodded but didn't release the tight hold he had on the sides of his seat.

The Sikanni Chief, flowing east and north to the Fort Nelson River, looked more like a swamp. Uncle Matthew said that every year the brown muskeg-draining water flooded across the flat land, picking up driftwood and piling it in dams, creating new channels through forest. Flying low over the water, we could see where the soil had been washed from the tree roots, killing them. Some trees stood straight, others leaned at odd angles like grey-haired old men. "Below us is the Valley of Ghosts," Uncle Matthew hollered. "It can be tricky landing when there's not enough water. You really have to watch for gravel bars and driftwood."

He circled until he spotted a clear back channel. We came flying in upriver, hit the water with a whump, and headed into shore near the camp. A man caught the tie rope I threw to him and pulled us in.

"I've got your newest mill hands here," Uncle Matthew said.

"Oh yeah. Otto told me we're hiring schoolboys now," the man said. "What next? Girls in pink dresses?"

I felt my fists clench and, before I knew it, I'd rushed at him. Uncle Matthew held me back. "Cut it out, both of you. Use your energy to unload some cargo."

Bugs gave me a quick look of sympathy, but I ignored it.

Two more men came to help us unload the plane, and nothing further was said. We'd brought out an order for the camp: kegs of nails and bolts so work could begin on proper buildings, and flour, sugar, powdered milk, and eggs.

"Where's the coffee? Tea? We're drinking swamp water out here!"

"Bad news, boys," Uncle Matthew said. "It's rationed now for the duration of the war."

The language that greeted that news made my face go hot. I'd heard lots of swearing at the mill, and Dad sometimes let out a few good cuss words when we were out in the bush, but these guys beat all. I wondered where Otto had picked up this crew.

Uncle Matthew gave me a look to remind me of his warning that this wouldn't be easy. When he left, I'd have just one friend at the Sikanni Chief camp — Bugs — and I didn't see how he'd be much help to me if this bunch turned against me.

If I thought the mill at Charlie Lake was shaganappi, this one was indescribable. Logging trails, pushed through the bush with bulldozers, had become canals of churned-up, half-frozen muskeg. A pilot crew of a dozen men had set up the mill and were housed in tents. Even the cookshack was in a tent, with the food cache high up on stilts to keep it safe from marauding animals.

Yet the sawmill was going crazy trying to keep up with the need for cut logs, six-by-six trusses, and deck planking for soon-to-be-built bridges, as the 341st Engineers were surveying now between Fort St. John and Fort Nelson.

We threw our bedrolls and packsack — and Bugs's valise — into the tent indicated by Mr. Knapp, and came back to the mess tent to get our job orders. Bugs knew roughly what his jobs would be, but my first assignment came as a complete surprise.

As it was noon, we ate first, at long sawhorse tables outside. I was given a chipped enamel plate with a cup to match, a crooked fork, and a knife with a twist at the end from someone apparently using it as a screwdriver.

We listened to the conversation buzzing around us. Two men who had just hauled out a load of lumber had lots to say about the building of the Alcan. "Army men are climbing the blasted trees like sailors in a crow's nest — to figure out which way to build the road!" one said.

"They don't know beans about muskeg," the second man added. "They've ordered bulldozers to cut through the top layer. Then they wonder why they're left with a water-filled moat. They try to ditch it, but that don't work. So they're laying logs across, like corduroy, and building the roadbed over that."

Mr. Knapp talked to Uncle Matthew, not to Bugs or me, as if we were beneath notice. "We're low on grub," he said. "The stuff you brought out from Fort Nelson is the first fresh food these men have had. And we're right out of meat."

"Why don't you get someone to go hunting?" Uncle Matthew asked.

"Can't spare a man. Have to get the contracts out before this muskeg swallows up our roads."

"You're not going to get much work out of hungry men," Uncle Matthew said mildly.

Mr. Knapp grunted and concentrated on his plate.

The food looked awful. Canned beef like they issue to the army: colourless canned vegetables and green things that looked like pigweed, and potatoes floating in grey, lumpy gravy. The men were working ten-and twelve-hour days on poor grub in the cold sleet or drizzling rain of an early spring in the middle of absolutely nowhere, and now they were hiring kids, when what they really needed was a hunter. I caught Mr. Knapp's eye. "I can hunt," I said.

"You'd shoot your foot off!"

"Don't underestimate this kid," said Uncle Matthew.

Mr. Knapp sat back, looking at me critically. "Yeah, maybe Jed's kid's not total deadwood."

I waited for Otto Knapp's little brain to get into gear, to recall how hard I'd been working for him down south.

"Naw, we need you here at the mill. We need a real hunter for this job, one who won't miss. The game's been overhunted. All this road action has scared the survivors up into the hills." Otto called over to a man sitting on a tree stump, eating alone. "Hey, got a job for you." The man looked up, but made no move. "Yeah, you! I want you to get some meat for this camp."

The man snapped to attention like he'd been given a prize. A grin came over his face.

"Right, boss," he said. "I'll need a grubstake, horses, ammunition."

"Get it together this afternoon and leave first thing in the morning," Mr. Knapp said. "And take this greenhorn along. He may be some good for packin'."

To my surprise, he indicated Bugs. Oh, boy.

I walked down to the river to say good-bye to Uncle Matthew. He seemed anxious about leaving me. I wanted to hop on the plane and fly away with him, but I couldn't ask. He'd agree with the others that I was a baby.

I awoke at five o'clock the next morning with a funny feeling that things weren't right. Light rain patted the roof of the tent, background music to the snores of the men. I lay still, letting my eyes adjust to the light. A shadow stood at the end of my bed.

"A bear! A bear!" I shouted.

The men jumped up at the same time, getting caught up in bedrolls. The bear, shocked at this sudden action, gave a grunt and ran back outside. He scrambled up the poplar tree holding our ridgepole, shaking men out of the tent like raisins from a bag.

"Get it down!" one man shouted.

"Get it down yourself!" another answered.

A keening wail came from under the blankets of the cot next to mine. Only Bugs's wide eyes showed, and they held a look of pure terror.

As I ran out, I heard a boom! as a shot blasted past my head. Mr. Knapp, running toward the tent, flung himself onto the ground. Blood smeared his upraised hand. One of the men had grabbed my gun and was wildly trying to pump another cartridge in it to get another shot at the bear, who had thumped down from the tree and was now running dazedly toward us. The fool had used the lower barrel, the .410 shotgun, good for birds! It was lucky that Mr. Knapp was as far away as he was. Any closer and the pellets wouldn't have separated — and he'd be dead.

"Give me my gun," I said quietly to the man, who was shaking as panic set in.

He handed it over.

I aimed the upper .22 barrel, waiting until I could get a clean shot at the bear's head or neck. One shot. The bear went down. I'd got it behind the knob on the top of its head. It started to rise. I fired again, another head shot. It rolled over, dead.

Mr. Knapp sat up and wiped his face, smearing blood all over himself. He was fighting mad. "You're fired!" he yelled at the guy who'd taken my gun. "And you! And you!" until I was the only one still on staff. "And *you're* crew boss!" he said pointing to me, his eyes sparking, "as soon as you and Yukon Jack skin out this black devil. The men can eat bear stew until they look like bears!"

I heard a strange noise from inside the tent. Sounded like Bugs was losing his last three meals, all at once. Boy, I could hardly wait to get out of here!

The men, oblivious at that moment to Bugs's problems, were standing outside in shocked silence.

"You're all rehired," Mr. Knapp gasped. "Except for the SOB who shot me!" He thumped back to the cookshack.

I stuck my head into the tent. "Better get this cleaned up, Bugs. Then meet me in the cookshack." He nodded, his eyes hollow and dull in his miserable face.

I watched as Otto Knapp picked the pellets out of his hand and swabbed the wounds with iodine. I gave him some help wrapping it up. When he'd had his cup of coffee, and Bugs had joined us, Otto grunted for us to come with him to meet Yukon Jack.

"The kids here'll be your hunting partners tomorrow."

Yahoo! I was getting out of this hole and going hunting, too!

Yukon Jack stuck out his hand to shake ours. "Howdy, boys," he said. "Nice shooting back there."

"Thanks."

I liked him right away. He had shaggy black hair streaked with grey, a beard, and sharp brown eyes. His front teeth, all he had, were long and brown as a beaver's. He looked like an old mountain man from the gold-rush days in his plaid wool shirt, black pants, leather boots, and stained cowboy hat.

"Well, get your skinning knives ready, boys. We've

got some butchering to do. Then we'll saddle up and vamoose!"

I wasn't about to tell him that Bugs had never handled a gun before, let alone a skinning knife, and had got sick at the sight of my dead bear.

Or that I'd never ridden a horse.

Yukon Jack and I skinned out the bear while Bugs got our grub together. Jack handed me the rifle I was to use on our hunt — a 300 Savage. Mine was not usually good for large game.

When we were ready to go, Yukon Jack secured the gear onto the packhorses with expert diamond hitches and began to saddle his horse. He pointed to the harness — tack — I was to put on my horse. I grabbed a blanket and saddle, trying to see, from the corner of my eye, how to tighten and knot the belly strap, which Yukon Jack called the cinch.

"Here." Yukon Jack came over and gave my horse a quick jab in the belly with his knee. The horse drew in a breath, and Jack quickly tightened the cinch a full two inches. "They blow themselves up," he said. "You'd a been riding upside down if your saddle had been that loose." His voice was low and pleasant, not harsh like Knapp's. He looked over at Bugs, who was obviously at a loss. "Here, boy," Yukon Jack said. "I just hope you're in good enough shape to stand the ride. Now, let's get some chow and get outa this place."

We ate quickly, leaving camp as the men were shuffling out to the mill, looking browned-off at the world.

When we were finally on the trail, I watched as Yukon Jack casually stuffed tobacco into a paper with one hand to make a smoke. He looked over at Bugs and me. "Smoke?"

"No, I don't," I said.

Bugs didn't even answer, as if opening his mouth would interfere with his concentration and he'd fall off.

His knuckles were white they were clenched so tightly around the saddle horn. And the horse was only walking.

Rain fell gently, misting the river valley. The cold clear smell of spring was in the air. The trail narrowed so we rode in single file, Yukon Jack first, then Bugs, me next, and the packhorse last. I laughed when I thought of Bugs's wish to ride a packhorse. After riding for an hour, my legs felt like they were no longer joined to my body. Every muscle in my inner thighs ached, and the back of the saddle rubbed my tailbone. I constantly shifted my weight to change the pressure points.

The rain stopped, and the sun tried to burn through the mist. Jack and I both scanned the bush for signs of moose, deer, or caribou.

We stopped to make lunch at a small clearing. I swung my right leg over the saddle, took my left foot from the stirrup and jumped to the ground. My knees buckled, and I almost collapsed. Jack looked over and laughed. "You'll get used to it," he said. "The first day is the worst." We looked over at Bugs, who seemed to be in a daze. "C'mon, boy," Yukon Jack said, and helped him down as if he were a lady.

I smiled in spite of the pain. It was such a relief to be honest about not knowing everything. I hadn't had that privilege since we'd left the trapline.

I headed for the horses to get our food from the panniers. Bugs took over the cooking, which was okay with Yukon Jack and me. Even though he'd not likely had much experience cooking over an open fire, he seemed to get the hang of it quickly, and his pancakes and beans tasted great.

We rode all day without seeing any big game but did come upon a mother fox and her kits playing on the rocks, chasing mice. A porcupine waddled off the path as we rounded a bend. Swimming our horses across a river, we saw beaver playing along the edge, smacking their tails in warning as we approached. We made a lean-to "wickiup" camp that night. Neither of us were in any hurry to end our "holiday," as Mr. Knapp had called it.

In mid-afternoon of the second day we spotted the tracks of two moose and followed them to a slough. One bull smelled us. He lifted his head, gave a snort, and started up the bank on the opposite side. Jack and I identified our targets, lifted our rifles, took careful aim, and fired. Both moose fell dead to the ground. I heard a noise behind the trees and looked back. Bugs was losing his lunch again.

Yukon Jack and I rode over to the bulls and cut their throats. It took the rest of the day to dress them and pack the meat onto the horses. Bugs stayed away, and we didn't say anything, just let him sit on the river bank and plan our supper. He helped pack, although I could tell it took every ounce of strength — inner and outer — to do it.

"The North is a pretty tough place," he said, as we were riding home.

"Any chechako can expect to get pushed around a bit at first," Yukon Jack replied. "Just ride it out."

"And you *are* kind of goofy sometimes," I said. I felt sort of smart, like I was as seasoned a Northerner as Yukon Jack, even though the mill hands might not see me that way — yet.

Again I drove the skid horses, hauled the water, and worked in the mill. I felt sorry for the horses here. They'd been brought in from the outside and had a hard time with the mosquitos and black flies. In the evenings they'd run in circles, switching their tails and shaking their manes as they tried to get away from the pests. We made smoke smudges from green wood to keep the insects away, but that didn't help all that much, and the horses couldn't sleep under netting the way we did. They were overworked, like the men. But the men could quit and walk out, take a vacation, tell off the boss.

In the evenings some of the men would play cribbage or poker, but they generally ignored Bugs and me, until Bugs showed them he knew games to play with cards beyond their imagination. He told them he was studying to be a magician. "Let me show you the Unseen Passage! Bet you don't know how I make this red king go from one pack to the other and end up between two black queens!" The men got interested and gave him a kind of grudging respect from then on.

They let him get in on their cribbage games, and he suggested they play for a penny a point, until he was taking their money every night, sometimes skunking or even double-skunking his opponents. Then he'd turn around and lose most of his profits to Yukon Jack, a crib expert. After a while, we all just played for fun.

One night when Bugs and I were playing a game of crib, I came right out and asked him if he had a girlfriend.

His face flushed crimson. "Well, I write to a couple of girls," he said. "I haven't actually met them yet."

"How'd you start writing to them then?"

His blush seemed to come in waves. "Ads in the paper for pen pals."

"Oh. I might have a pen pal. Loretta wants me to write."

"Hey, good going! She seemed nice."

"Yeah." Why did my face feel like it was flaming?

"I was going to ask you," Bugs said. "Would you mind taking my picture tomorrow? I haven't got a recent one. I told Frances I'd send her a photo."

"Sure."

"Do you have a girlfriend back in Edmonton?"

"Oh, yeah. Several. But they all got too serious. I wanted to do some travelling first."

"So you came up here?"

"Yeah. I wanted to get some adventuring in before I settle down. And I guess I am."

"Me, too," I said. "But I'm going to go to flying school in Washington, like my uncle did."

"Won't that take a lot of money?"

"I guess so. I'd better start saving special for it. Mom was going to put my wages in a trust account, but she sure wouldn't let me spend any of it on flying lessons!"

"Here." Bugs handed me an empty Players "flat-fifty" tin. "It makes a good bank. Start now. And you'll make it, Jay. I just know you will."

It felt good to have someone near my age to talk to, who didn't laugh at me. Bugs was my first real friend.

When I'd proved myself at falling, skidding, canting and tailing, and even calculating lumber for the Johnson bar, Mr. Knapp promoted me to driving a Cat and a truck.

"Dogs, horses, trapping — they're all going to be things of the past, boy," Mr. Knapp said. "I'm doin' you a real favour. You learn to operate and repair machinery, drive heavy-duty trucks and Cats, you'll be set for life. Get a job anywhere."

"I'm not working in a sawmill forever. Or being a Cat skinner. Or a truck driver. Or a grease monkey."

"Oh? And what has his royal highness decided to be?" Mr. Knapp asked, his eyes narrowing.

"A bush pilot."

"You're a fool, kid," he said, spitting on the ground as he stomped off. "And so am I. For hiring a camp full of stupid know-nothing greenhorn dreamers."

14

Moving up the Road

On June 5 the United States declared war on Bulgaria, Hungary, and Romania. Next, we heard that the Germans had seized Tobruk in North Africa, then the British halted the Germans at El Alamein. The men added more pins to a map in the cook tent.

It had been a wet spring. On June 7 four-and-a-half inches of rain washed out most of our temporary culverts and bridges. But by July 1 the temperature shot to ninety-nine above. We were punching the defence road through in awful conditions, knowing we played just a small part in the real action of the war.

Dad sent word that the mill was set up at the Liard, near what was to be Mile 500 of the Alcan Highway. Mr. Knapp was away so we didn't get a chance to say good-bye to him.

We shook hands with Yukon Jack and promised to keep up our crib playing.

The Norseman thudded up the Sikanni River, and we were airborne. As we flew toward the west, we could see several small forest fires that had been started by lightning, or careless construction workers. It made me angry that people could come into the wilderness with so little respect.

When we stopped over in Fort Nelson, the town was buzzing.

"Canadian Pacific Airlines has regular air service here now," Uncle Matthew informed us. "They've bought out Yukon Southern Air, and some small bush airlines who'd developed the airport."

All the equipment that had come in — Cats, bulldozers, scrapers, trucks, and large aircraft — had changed the look of the place completely, in both good and bad ways. Rough trails through the bush led to clusters of shacks. Old fuel barrels and broken-down pieces of equipment lay everywhere. Airplanes were coming and going as if Fort Nelson were the centre of the world. No longer was the arrival of boats or floatplanes the most exciting thing to happen to the village.

After Bugs and I helped Uncle Matthew unload the cargo that was to stay in Fort Nelson, we went to the Nite Owl Cafe for a meal. Uncle Matthew was picking at his food, nervous.

"What's the matter?" I asked.

He took a deep breath. "Jay, there's been some trouble. You should know about it before you get to your dad's camp." He looked from Bugs to me.

"Hey, I'll leave if you want to discuss personal stuff," Bugs said.

"No, it's okay. Stay," I said.

Uncle Matthew hesitated again, until I thought I would punch him if he didn't get it out.

"I met a guy who owned a gold mine out of Fairbanks and introduced him to your dad. Jed knows gold mining. They got on pretty good, and the fellow said he might take in a couple of partners. We got took in, all right."

"What happened?" My heart was pounding to beat the band. I just knew I was going to hear something awful.

"Okay, here it is. We had to raise some capital, fast. Your dad and I got into a card game. A fellow there operates the only legal gambling house in B.C. and, well, we lost. A lot."

"You and *Dad* gambled? But Dad *hates* — "

"I know. But this seemed like a chance to really get somewhere. Your dad's been thinking about buying out Knapp and forming a partnership with you. And I . . . well, pilots are always hearing of mineral claims. We fly prospectors all over — I thought it was a good chance to invest. Now — " he gave a hollow-sounding laugh, "we're broke. And we'd have been broke either way — gold's not selling now because of the war. And that's all there is to tell."

"But the mill?"

"Jed and Otto have split their partnership. Your dad owns only the Liard mill now. Your mom's wages paid to get the equipment and crew up there, and you're going to have to grubstake the operation until some cash comes in."

"Why did he do it? Why did you — " I couldn't look at him.

"We made a mistake." He looked so ashamed, my hero. His face was flushed, and he couldn't meet my eyes. Neither could Bugs. "Your dad wanted to give you a better life, a decent home instead of just a shack in the bush. He gambled, and lost."

"I wish we were still in our *shack* in the bush! We were richer then. Before *you* came! You brought the war to us, all right! We've been doing nothing but fighting ever since."

"Jay, he — we — were only — "

"And gambling! Dad's worse than Braden — he's a phoney! And so are you!" I held out my hands, all calloused and criss-crossed with cuts and imbedded with slivers, the hands of a man. I felt tears and was so ashamed and hurt I just wanted to get out of there. I jumped up, accidentally catching the table. The dishes rattled and food spilled, causing everyone to look. My face felt like it was burning up.

"He did it for you," I heard Uncle Matthew say, but I was gone.

Bugs followed me outside, where I stood leaning against the wall of the building.

"I'm not going up to the Liard," I said. "I'll work on the highway. I can drive a truck for someone — "

"Jay, you don't even have a licence! You've never driven a truck."

"I'll learn! I can do anything . . . work in the bush. I'll run away, like you did!"

"It wasn't hard for me to run away — there was no one to say good-bye to. Your mother and Jody need you. Think of your family."

My thoughts churned like a maelstrom on the Sikanni Rapids. I hated everyone. I hated this highway. All it was doing for the North was bringing in crooks like Bean Trap Braden, cranks like the men at the Sikanni camp, people who wanted to get rich quick, never mind the country, never mind the animals or the people that might get in the way. Never mind the trappers or the Indians whose territories were being ripped up by the road, the game animals being shot to feed thousands of men in camps strung through fifteen hundred miles of wilderness. Thousands of trees were being logged, forever scarring the forests. Permafrost and muskeg ripped up, to never heal again. I wiped my eyes with the backs of my hands. Bugs didn't seem to notice.

"I want to help," he said. "You and your family have done everything for me. It's my turn to do something for you."

I couldn't answer him. I thought of the sawmill at the Liard. I knew the timber lease we'd got was good, and the highway would provide contracts. We'd make money all right.

"We can't take your money, Bugs," I said. "But maybe if you'd work for a percentage of the profits — "

"Sure! You bet!"

Uncle Matthew came wandering outside.

I took a deep breath. "Uncle Matt, if it's my money that says whether this mill at the Liard goes or not, then it's my mill, too. I'd like a say in how things are run."

"You're telling this to the wrong man, Jay. Let's fly up to the Liard."

"I want to write it down, my part in the deal. All legal-wise," I said.

"I can help with that," Bugs said. "I worked in a bank. I know about legal stuff."

"Okay, let's talk to Dad."

This time, I didn't ask Uncle Matthew if I could take over Nellie's controls for a while. And he didn't offer.

We flew to the new camp, and I got my first glimpse of what I was trying to get a part of: a few tents, a couple of pieces of machinery, and a lease on miles of bush. Dad was waiting on the makeshift dock as we taxied in. He looked tired and kind of sick. Conda rushed up to greet me. Dad didn't. I walked over to him, said, "Hello, Dad," then, "I think we should have a talk."

"Later."

"No, now."

Uncle Matthew spoke up. "Jed, I think you'd better."

Dad glared at Uncle Matthew. "I don't need any more advice from you!"

The look on Uncle Matthew's face said he wasn't about to take full blame for anything that had happened. I'd had time to calm down and didn't really blame either of them: it had happened, now we had to make the best of it. Just because I was a kid didn't mean I wasn't as smart as anybody else. I'd thought of Uncle Matthew as a hero, and he was — sometimes. And Dad as a grouch, and he was — sometimes. And I was a little bit like both of them.

We followed Dad into the cook tent. Bugs took out a piece of paper and a pencil.

"What's this?"

Bugs's face flamed.

"He's going to write down what we say," I explained. "What we agree to."

"Just a minute. Lilly!" Mom came over to the table. The two of them got up and went outside. When they came back in, Dad said, "Okay, we're all in this together."

"I want to help, too," Uncle Matthew said. "My flying's free."

Dad scowled, but I could tell the worst was over.

"Well, Jay," he said when we'd come to terms on a work and partnership split, "you're now part owner of a T-120 Chrysler mill, a saw, roller, and carriage." He waved toward some pieces of machinery sitting out in the yard. "And there's your Model D 'Poppin' John Deer tractor and your old Ford three-ton truck. How do you feel?"

"Okay," I said.

"Then you're a worse gambler than me." It was the closest Dad would ever come to admitting what he'd done.

When Uncle Matthew was ready to leave, he held out his hand to Dad. Dad shook it but kept his eyes down.

Then he stalked off to the mill. I didn't say anything as I walked to the plane with Uncle Matthew.

"I'll be working out of Fairbanks the next couple of months," he said. "You've got your hands full here, but I know you'll make a go of it. You need me, put in a radio call to the airport at Whitehorse or Fairbanks. They'll know where I am."

"When we're done here, I want to finish school in Fairbanks," I said. "Then I'd like your help to get enrolled in a flying school."

"I'll do what I can, Jay. I owe you one." He put his hand on my shoulder.

I was beginning to realize how alike Dad and his brother really were: never back up, never say sorry, but make up for it in other ways.

He hopped onto the pontoon, up into the plane, and with a roar of the 550-horsepower Pratt and Whitney engine, Midnight Smith and Nellie were gone.

I went down to the machine shed where Dad was sorting through some greasy-looking parts. There was one more thing I had to get off my mind before we plunged full speed ahead into this family business.

"Dad," I said. "I met a girl. In Fort Nelson."

Dad's face showed a trace of interest.

"Her name is Loretta Braden."

Dad's look froze.

"Her father is William J. Braden."

"Bean Trap." Dad stared as if he'd seen a grizzly bear.

"I know the story. You told me some, and Uncle Matt told me the rest," I said. "The miners at Eagle think you're a hero."

"Not Matt's business to tell you anything!"

"Well, I guess he had to because I wanted to go out and visit Loretta in Weasel City. He wouldn't take me. I don't know what to do, Dad. I said I'd write to her. Like a pen pal."

"I wouldn't advise it."

"But you and Bean Trap . . . it's over, isn't it? You paid."

"Not to his account."

"But I really like her."

"Then suit yourself. Write to your girl."

My girl. That sounded kind of nice.

I went to look over the camp: scraggly tents, a mill, a wood shanty called an engine room, machine shed, slab pile, our timber lease standing dark and green as far back into the hills as I could see. I thought of Dad leaving his wealthy home in Seattle when he was fifteen to come to Alaska and of Mom leaving her parents to marry him and move to his gold claim at Eagle, then going back to Dawson City while Dad served his sentence. Was she ashamed? Did she have to make excuses to her parents and friends? I recalled our move to Fairbanks and to the Tanana River. And the arrival of my uncle, the Wolf Man, who brought us news of America being in the war. Dad never backed down from a challenge, and neither would I. But how could I write to Loretta?

I'd have to talk it over with Bugs. He'd help me straighten out my thoughts on this romance thing. I was sure glad I had a friend.

I went back to the cook tent for my bag and bedroll, then found a spot to sleep in one of the hot, fly-infested tents.

15

A Short Madness

30 Shells in 40 Minutes Fall on Estevan Point
on the West Coast of Vancouver Island by
"Undersea Raider."

The Highway crawled toward us from both directions.
Wilderness that had never known the tracks of man was
being churned up at a rate of four miles per day. The
road wound up mountains to a height of four thousand
feet at Summit Lake and plunged to one thousand feet
above sea level near Fort Nelson. It leapt rivers and
skirted lakes, followed old prospectors' trails, switched
back and forth from the Yukon to B.C., and finally into
Alaska. The Whitehorse to Fairbanks section ran
through our old trapping territory at the Tanana River.
The Alcan would end at the Delta Junction, Mile 1,422.
From there they were going to use the Richardson
Highway to Fairbanks, Mile 1,520.

Now that the long daylight hours of summer were
here, highway crews were working twenty-four-hour
days, and so were we.

By the middle of July, the weather was one of the least

worries at Liard camp. We had no money. We had ratty machinery. Food was running low. We were committed to contracts that I didn't know how we were going to fulfil. Half-a-dozen men were working for us: four men on the mill — canter, sawyer, and two tail sawyers to handle the lumber; two fallers; and Dad, Mom, Jody, and me.

Dad and I had made a peace of sorts. We hardly talked except for business. I didn't like it much. I remembered when I was little, Dad had taught me bush craft and told me stories of the people and animals in the North. I wanted to know more about Dad's early years, especially now that Uncle Matthew had come into our lives. Before that, it had been hard to believe Dad wasn't always an adult. When did things change? When did Dad become quiet and cranky if I so much as asked him a question about his past?

"Your dad's just nervous these days," Mom said when I asked her about his attitude.

Maybe, I thought, it was because of Braden. But was he still a threat? Was Dad afraid that, because of me, Braden might find us? And even if he did, I couldn't see Dad backing down to him — he hadn't before and he still had his strong spirit, which I'd seen evidence of in Fort St. John.

One day Dad said he wanted me to pair up with him to fell timber. I was glad we would be really working as partners. It might give us a chance to talk. We felled trees all morning, using a Swede saw.

"Time to stop for lunch," Dad said, mopping his forehead with his red handkerchief.

I grabbed the saw and headed to a tall pine. "One more," I said, taunting him.

"Okay, but let's hurry it up. I'm hungry."

I started sawing, faster and faster, me pushing him until the tree was ready to go. We pulled the saw out and stood back. Suddenly branches crashed down all around us! I leapt and rolled out of the way. I heard Dad scream in agony. As soon as I untangled myself, I crawled over to him. "Are you okay?" I called, through the branches. He was pinned. All he could do was grunt a response.

"Oh, Dad, I'm sorry!" I could see that a branch was holding the tree trunk off his body, all that had saved him from being crushed. I bucked and limbed the tree, hearing Dad's harsh breathing beneath the debris, wondering if his ribs had been broken and his lungs punctured. Finally I rolled the tree off him. He lay there, looking at the sky for a moment, then slowly worked his way, with me helping him, to a sitting position.

"I *told* you it was time to quit!" he panted. Sweat ran off his forehead and down the sides of his face; his hair was full of leaves and dirt.

"I didn't see that poplar tree! Where did it come from?"

"Dead one. The pine was holding it up." He stopped to catch his breath. "Guess I shoulda told you to check for sleepers like that."

I could see now that the poplar tree had been intertwined in the pine boughs. The force of the pine falling had yanked it out of the ground, and it had come crashing down. I couldn't stand the thought of how close I'd come to seriously injuring, or killing, my own father.

"Dad, I'm so sorry."

He looked up at me, a slight smile on his face. "Don't worry, son. We're all allowed one mistake. Now, give me a hand to get out of this nest, and let's eat lunch!"

My relationship with Dad improved after that incident, so sometimes good things can come from bad. I still felt, though, that Dad's anger could flare up again. Dad talked about our future in the sawmill business now that the North was being opened up with the highway construction. I just couldn't tell him that I'd asked Uncle Matt for his help to get into flying school.

In the evenings when it was raining we sat around in the cookshack, drinking a coffee substitute made from chicory while we played cards. Sometimes we sang when Mom had the time or energy to play the harmonium. Bugs had bought a guitar and a set of correspondence lessons from a guy leaving camp. They included a coloured paper chart to insert on the neck of the guitar to show where to place his fingers for the chords. Even with the chart it took him forever to find the next chord. When he played, singers had to pause and wait for him to grope for the right positions on the guitar neck.

"Bugs is trying to teach himself something," Mom said, "and you should be, too. You've been shirking your schoolwork."

"Mom, I don't have time right now. I'll catch up later."

"You're getting too big for your britches."

Bugs was also still working on his magician's course from the same correspondence school. He'd get out his deck of cards, and I'd be stuck as the audience. His tricks didn't always work, and then he'd analyze them in front of me until there was no magic left.

I had been kind of important to Bugs, first for rescuing him, then for teaching him about the North. Now we were kept busy working ten to twelve hours a day, and when we were free he'd work on his lessons. Mom was going crazy cooking for the camp, with Bugs and two-year-old Jody as helpers. Dad was carrying the worries of the world on his shoulders, as usual. And, although I was working as hard as the rest of them, I felt restless and lonely. It seemed I had nothing special to offer anybody.

I thought a lot about Loretta. I sure hoped if we got settled somewhere that I'd run into her again. One day Bugs said, "Why don't you get brave and write her a letter? Your dad doesn't care. What are you afraid of?" So I did, addressing the envelope to Loretta Braden, Weasel City, B.C.

Dear Loretta,

Here I am at our sawmill camp on the Liard River just a few miles away from where the new highway is going through. I am part owner of this mill, so I hope I get rich! Ha! Ha!

I really liked meeting you. Your hair is beautiful and so are you. Don't ever cut it.

There's not much to write about here, lots of trees and stuff. Bugs says "hi." He's studying to be a magician. Maybe he can make you appear instead of a rabbit! Ha! Ha!

Hi to Teddy.

Your friend,
Jay Smith

On the eighteenth of July, when the temperature was over a hundred, Jody got sick. She became delirious with fever, and there seemed to be nothing we could do for her. She'd call for me, but when I knelt by her bed, she'd look at me and howl in fear, like she was seeing monsters. Dad drove the old three-ton truck to a highway work camp to radio for a plane. Jody's nightmares stayed throughout the day, until Mom was near panic.

That night we heard thunder rolling in, and the sky turned as black as the inside of a goat. But the plane made it! Bugs and I ran down to the beach. The plane landed upstream and bucked toward the bank. It was the Norseman.

Before the propeller had stopped I grabbed a rope and gave one end to Bugs. Then I waded out and clambered onto the front of the pontoon. I almost lost my balance in the wind but managed to catch the loop over the cleat. Bugs pulled the plane in and secured the rope to a tree.

Uncle Matthew jumped to shore. He looked like a ghost. "Jay, *never* come near a plane when the engine's still running! One whack with the prop and your head would have gone flying into the river!"

I laughed, but it came out as a nervous cackle. The doctor hurried up the bank toward the camp, shaking his head at my stupidity. Bugs turned white, and swallowed over and over; he couldn't get a word out.

"I came out to save a life, not to destroy one," Uncle Matthew added.

"Don't tell Mom or Dad," I said, as we followed the doctor. "They've got enough to worry about." I could feel my face flaming.

Bugs looked at me sympathetically, but I couldn't meet his eyes.

"Some mail came for you," Uncle Matthew said casually, handing me a letter. I felt my face turn even redder when I saw a pink envelope. I shoved it into my pocket. "Don't tell," I repeated.

Jody had tonsillitis. The doctor helped Mom with her, and when the storm let up they left for Fort Nelson. Two of our crew quit and went with them. Dad still wasn't talking much to Uncle Matthew. He gave him an abrupt greeting, then stayed at the mill until just before he saw us walking back to the plane. Then he came down to the landing, gave Mom a real hard hug, kissed Jody's hot little head, and nodded a good-bye to Uncle Matt.

After they left, I stayed by the riverbank to read my letter.

Dear Jay,

Is that your real name? Does it stand for something longer, like Jacob, or were you named for a bird? Ha ha. Anyway, I think it's nice.

We are living in a little settlement of about ten cabins.

There is no school, so I don't think we'll be here very long. The men are mostly trappers, and the women and kids are Indians and don't speak English very well. I don't know what Dad does here, some kind of business, but he works at night. Teddy and I are kind of bored. We can't make any noise in the day when Dad is sleeping, and it's kind of scary to be alone at night when he's out doing his work. It's a funny place. No one talks to us.

I hope you're working hard at the sawmill, building lots of muscles, ha ha.

Please write again. It was so nice to get a letter.

Yours till the mountain peaks and sees the salad dressing!

Your friend,
Loretta.

I showed the letter to Bugs, but his mind seemed to be on other things.

"What's wrong?" I said. "Jealous?"

"No, of course not. I've got a girl. Frances and I are writing — I got a letter today, too."

"So, what's the problem?"

"She wants me to come back to the city. She says it's too dangerous here."

"Go on! Deep down she probably thinks you're really

swell and the city guys are boring. And what would I do without you?"

He smiled a bit, then said, "To tell you the truth, Jay, I've been thinking of joining up for service overseas. I nearly got on your uncle's plane. I came that close."

"Well, next time see me first. I'll talk some sense into you. This is a chance of a lifetime to earn some good money, and you're helping the war effort right here. You join the army, they'll have you sitting in an office, doing accounting stuff. Anybody could do that."

"Don't be so sure, Jay." The tone of his voice got cold. "There's things even *you* know nothing about."

Bugs went to the cookshack to prepare supper, and I followed him. Dad came in, poured a cup of chicory coffee, and sat down.

"Until Mom gets back, Bugs will be camp cook," Dad said. "You can take over some of his odd jobs."

"Odd jobs! Oh yeah, in my spare time I'll do Bugs's 'odd jobs.'"

"There's always something new a person can learn."

"Yeah. Right." I glared at both of them.

"If you keep your nose clean, you can take over this mill completely."

"This shaganappi outfit? Forget it!"

Dad looked as if I'd punched him in the gut. Bugs turned away and started peeling spuds.

"I'm not staying around the bush. I'm going to be a pilot," I finished, lamely.

"Whatever you think is fair, Jay."

Dad got up, threw the remaining coffee into the slop bucket, and strode out to the mill.

16

Bugs

ALASKA ROAD WORKERS CREATE NEW
BOOM TOWN OF "LITTLE AMERICA"
IN FORT ST. JOHN

"Alaska and the Canadian North country is one
hive of industry," said Air Minister C. G. Power.
"You have no idea just what activity is going on
up there — and I can't tell you."

On August 14 troops pushed the road across the Liard
River. The Carcross-Watson and Muncho-Watson lakes
crews met at Teslin on August 24. The 95th Engineers
located to Mile 105 (Tanana Crossing), and the 18th
Engineers located to Mile 255, west of Whitehorse.

We suffered through a spell of two weeks without
rain. The winds blew hot and dry and turned the under-
brush to tinder. Fires were reported throughout the
district. Some were started by lightning, some by man.
We warned our crew not to smoke or light campfires —
which meant no hot food for the fallers in the bush. Slab
piles couldn't be burned, and sparks from tractors or
other machinery were a constant threat. We tried to

keep our fuel barrel leakage to a minimum, but there's always some.

Dust coated the standing timber, as well as our piled logs, causing saw blades to dull before half a shift was over. The work slowed, increasing production costs. Dad was jumpy as a cricket.

"I don't like the air," he said. "It's got a bad smell." He climbed in the truck to drive some lumber to the army camp.

"You look beat, Dad. Have a rest. I'll take the load in for you."

"Get serious."

"Then I'm coming with you. Bugs, you, too."

"I got pies — " Bugs said.

"Never mind. We might need your help to change a flat. This road's nothing but dust and boulders."

Ruts, formed after the rain, had dried hard as concrete. Overloaded and unbalanced, we wound our way toward the highway in the loud, dusty, gear-grinding old truck.

At the highway we drove north until we reached the army crew constructing a bridge over the Liard River. We drove past some men eating outdoors at a long table. They looked like Martians. The army had issued them mosquito netting, which draped from their ranger hats and tucked into their collars. They'd flip up the nets, shovel in forkfuls of food, and quickly drop the netting, swearing as a fly or mosquito buzzed inside. When we stopped to unload, I saw the working men were dressed the same. Covered by the mosquito netting, they were pushing and pulling on cross-cut saws. Most had never used saws before and had no rhythm.

"We never seen flies like this! Y'all call 'em white stockings! Man, they don't even take off theah boots!

Just kick up a ruckus on ma neck, then go on to ma friends. They'ah monsters!"

One of the reasons I liked making deliveries up the highway was we were usually invited to the mess tent for a meal. The soldiers were always happy to talk to civilians, but they liked to tease us about living with the polar bears.

"You boys from up here?" one fellow asked Bugs and me.

"Yes — " Bugs said.

"I am but he's not," I said quickly. "He's from the city."

"I don't know how y'all can stand this confounded country! I'm a city boy myself and I can't *wait* to get back theah!"

I felt my face redden.

"I'm going out someday," I said. "To Seattle — to flying school."

"Better think about it, kid. What goes up, comes down."

"One just hit a mountain near Tuchodi Lake."

"And three B-26 bombers — Marauders — disappeared somewhere between Fort Nelson and Watson Lake on their way from Boise to Fairbanks."

"Following their leader."

"Typical armed forces manoeuvre."

"Okay in daylight."

"The poor boys don't know what it's like up here. They're used to coming in on radio beams. Leader gets lost, they all follow him."

"Yeah, another score for Uncle Sam's Million Dollar Valley."

"Where's that?" one fellow asked.

"Near Smith River," I said. "Named after my family."

The men laughed. "So you're claiming Uncle Sam's Millions?"

"Some Northern flyers are out helping the Air Force look for those bombers."

"Isn't easy. Camouflaged planes! In all this bush and rocks. They should be painted bright yellow."

"I bet you anything my Uncle Matthew is helping in the search. He wouldn't be afraid of the Valley," I said.

"I sure wish I had an uncle like Midnight Smith," Bugs said after the men had gone. "You're lucky."

"Well, maybe next time he comes I'll ask if you can go flying with us," I said, still embarrassed at how I'd tried to show off. "Maybe he'd teach you about the controls."

"Gosh, I'd like that! I've never flown a plane before," Bugs laughed.

"There's a couple of forest fires in the area," the sergeant told Dad. "Be careful you don't get cut off from your camp."

The sky was hazy grey with smoke and heat, and it hurt to breathe. I looked down at my shirt and was surprised to see bits of black stuff on my shoulders: ashes, carried by the wind over how many miles.

On our way back to camp we noticed smoke in the valleys. At our turn-off we headed into the haze.

"This trail's going to be fun." Dad was gripping the steering wheel so hard his knuckles were white. Bugs stopped whistling. I sat in the middle, squinting to keep my eyes from watering in the dry acrid air. It hurt to swallow.

"I'm sure our camp's not in danger," Dad said. "The wind's blowing this way."

He stepped on the gas, and the old Ford lunged forward. A rut caused me to fly up and hit my head on the roof. "Take it easy, Dad," I said.

"Gotta get past it. Hang on."

Now the fire could be seen on each side of the roadway, little flames leaping from bush to bush.

We wheeled around a sharp S-curve, and Dad began shifting down. The transmission screamed as it tried to slow three tons of truck. Suddenly we lurched like a jumping horse and were sent free-wheeling down the curve. Dad pumped frantically on the brake pedal. "The brakes are gone!" He pulled hard on the emergency, and we momentarily slowed, but our speed burned that brake out, too.

The truck raced out of control, ramming over ruts as we careened down curve after curve. Then a loud bang — "Front tire's blown!"

Bugs and I grabbed the dash and braced ourselves, staring at the steep curve before us and open sky beyond. The truck left the road, and we were airborne. Then everything happened in slow motion . . . the flames below us licking the tree tops; a raven flying up to meet us; the odometer showing seventy miles an hour; the grimace on Dad's face; and Bugs's whimper. There was a loud crash and the sound of glass breaking. My head exploded in a million lights, and then everything went dark.

"Jay!" Dad was leaning over, looking at me through the broken windshield. His face was black, and there was blood on his mouth. "Jay!" He shook me. "C'mon! We have to get out!" Dad pulled me out through the windshield and helped me to my feet. "Can you walk, son?"

"I think so."

"Then move! The truck's going to blow! I'll get Bugs."

The wind blew a cinder onto my neck. I could smell gas fumes. "Where is he?"

Bugs lay unmoving, half in and half out of the truck. Dad pulled at his shoulders, and then we saw that his foot was pinned between the door and a rock bank. Dad tried to lift the truck as I tugged. It moved, but not enough to free Bugs's foot. Bugs opened his eyes. "What happened?" He tried to sit up. "Get me out of here!"

"We are! We are!"

"Jay, I'll do it. You run!"

"Help me! Please!" Bugs clawed at the ground like a trapped animal, then fell back.

Dad grabbed his hunting knife from his belt sheath. He was choking from the smoke and smell of gas. He didn't seem to notice me anymore.

Bugs lifted his head and looked toward his trapped foot. "Go ahead," he whispered, and passed out.

Dad took his knife and cut through Bugs's pant leg. I could see the shattered bone sticking out between the calf and ankle. Dad ripped off his shirt and tied a tourniquet below Bugs's knee. "There's no hope of saving your foot, pal," Dad said softly. With sure strokes he cut it off. I turned away, and lost my lunch in the bush. When I looked back, Dad had picked Bugs up in his arms. "Run, Jay! Move!" he cried, and I ran.

The explosion knocked us to the ground. Parts of the truck flew through the air and crashed down all around us. I scrambled to my feet. Dad and Bugs were right behind me. I turned to help Dad with Bugs, but Dad carried him as if he weighed no more than Jody. We ran for a nearby creek, sliding down the bank into the water.

We stayed there until the fire passed. Bugs slipped in and out of consciousness.

"Will he be okay?" I asked.

"I hope so. He's young and strong. He hasn't lost too much blood."

My eyes were watering from the smoke-filled air. "What do you think started this fire?" I asked.

Dad gave a snort. "I think God started this one, a mix of lightning and dry timber."

"When the cabin burned, I thought at first Braden

had done it, because of you. Then this," I babbled. "This time it was because of me."

Dad raised his eyes to look into mine. "Don't you take on my burdens, son. You'll soon have enough of your own. Braden's a coward. But he got me in his own way."

"How?"

"The card game. It was his cronies running that show, I know that now. And I was trying to make a quick buck, just like all his other suckers."

"Dad," I said quickly, before I lost courage, "I wrote to Loretta."

"Figured you mighta."

"If Braden knew where you were, conned you into that game, it's because he saw my letter."

"Don't overestimate yourself. Stick to your own problems."

I had problems, all right. I didn't know how I was going to live with the fact that I'd pushed Bugs into coming with us. Just because I'd saved his life once didn't make me Bugs's boss. I'd been acting too important. Bugs's act of bravery, telling Dad to go ahead and do whatever he had to, was something I don't think I could have done. And I couldn't have cut his foot off, either.

When it was safe, we crawled onto the bank. Bugs was still unconscious, but his colour had come back a bit.

"He's in shock," Dad said. "Body's way of staying alive when the mind can't take it. We've got to keep him warm."

Dad had cut as low as possible, leaving a skin flap and a bit of muscle. I felt sick again just looking at it.

"He can get a wooden foot, can't he, Dad?"

Bugs started to stir and opened his eyes. "We made it," he said. He smiled weakly and raised himself up on his elbows, then, seeing his foot gone, he started to cry. Dad took Bugs in his arms. "You'll be okay, son, you'll be fine." He turned to me. "Go to camp, Jay. Get the men."

I started away, then stopped. "Dad?"

"Yeah."

"That was the bravest thing I've ever seen anyone do."

"You take care, son."

I clambered up the bank to the logging road. The fire was burning itself out in the valley. Our camp would be safe.

The crew carried Bugs back to camp on a stretcher. Someone radioed for help. An airplane and doctor arrived the next morning, but the pilot wasn't Uncle Matthew.

I went to pack Bugs's belongings. He'd made a home of his little corner of the tent. A photo of a lady wearing a dress with big shoulder pads and a hat shaped like a heart was propped up on his apple-box dresser. It was signed, "With love, Frances." Inside his dresser were course books and magic supplies: Chinese linking rings, silk scarves, coloured cards. He had magician's makeup, including false eyebrows and a moustache. Holding the moustache to my lip, I peered in his little tin mirror. I looked like Dad.

I put Bugs's belongings carefully into that silly old valise, packed his few clothes into a duffle bag, and picked up his guitar case. As I turned to leave I noticed a letter sticking out from under his pillow.

Dear Barry,

I was so pleased to receive your reply to my ad and to realize that men can be lonely, too. I think it is very interesting that you are mining gold in the North. If you find any, send some in the next letter!!

I didn't read any further. I folded the letter around the picture and tucked it into his bag.

When I was finished the men were already carrying Bugs to the airplane on a stretcher.

"You can go if you want, keep him company on the way down," Dad said.

"No, you need me here. I don't know how we're going to manage without Bugs. He really ran the show." I looked down at Bugs and winked. He winked back. His face blurred before my eyes.

"Be seeing you, buddy," Bugs said, his voice barely above a whisper. "Say hello to Loretta for me." He reached out his hand. I grabbed it and held on all the way to the airplane.

"I'm really going to miss you, pal."

"You're ever down in Edmonton, look me up. Maybe I'll be back at the bank on Jasper Avenue."

"I sure will." I finally let go of his hand.

"Maybe I'll play for dances, too," he said, indicating his guitar. I recalled him dancing the "Sailor's Hornpipe" at Easter, and I swallowed hard.

"Thanks, Jed. You guys saved my life . . . again. Tell Mrs. Smith I'll never forget her lovely face and nice music."

The men gently loaded the stretcher onto the airplane, the pilot and doctor climbed aboard, and they were gone.

17

Missing in Action

ALASKA HIGHWAY GROWS RAPIDLY

Every man works 12-hour shift

The Alcan, or the Road to Tokyo as some called it, was to be finished by fall. We didn't see how it could be possible, but on September 1, the 73rd Light Pontoon company crossed the Donjek River; 837 miles of road had been built in five and one-half months of work.

We bought another truck and kept going. Men were working to the north and south of us, so we hired more crew to get out the last contracts. Mom and Jody were back with us again. It sure changed the attitude of the camp when they were here.

Things were finally paying off.

I received another letter from Loretta. It was short and looked as if it had been written in a hurry. The envelope was smudged, as if she had been crying.

Dear Jay,

We are moving, right now. Teddy and I are packing as quickly as we can. Dad found your letter and got really angry. I told him you'd moved and were in Alaska again! He tore your letter up and said I couldn't write you anymore. We might be moving to Butte, Montana. I think Dad is in some kind of trouble here. I'll try to write again when we get settled.

Yours till the cowslips into the buttercup,
Loretta XXX OOO

All I could do now was wait until I heard from her again. I sure hoped I would.

On the first of October Dad and I delivered another load of planks to a camp twenty miles north of us. This troop had befriended an orphaned moose calf. Good thing they'd be out of here before it became an adult and came crashing through their tent. And the moose's days were numbered if it thought humans were its friends.

We stopped at the mess tent for supper. As we walked in, I overheard the latest news of the highway.

"Never would have believed it — twenty-fourth of September, the 35th Engineers met the 340th at Contact Creek."

"Where's that?

"Something over three hundred miles west of Fort Nelson. Well, that completes the southern part of this godforsaken road. We'll be out of here soon."

"Yeah, and on the twenty-eighth the first truck made it through from Dawson Creek to Whitehorse. Seventy-one hours of back-breaking driving. Averaged fifteen miles per hour over 1,030 miles."

"Wonder when they're going to find those lost bombers. This country gives me the creeps. Too wild."

A poster in the entry to the mess tent caught my eye.

MISSING: NORSEMAN NC-195N, LAST
SIGHTED EAST OF SMITH RIVER

SEPTEMBER 26, 1942, ON SEARCH AND
RESCUE MISSION. PILOT MATTHEW
"MIDNIGHT" SMITH OF FAIRBANKS.

"The Valley of Lost Planes!" I whispered.

I felt Dad's hand on my shoulder. I looked up. His face
was white.

"Maybe it's wrong. Maybe he's been found already."

But Dad seemed to not hear me. "That last time, he
came in for Jody, I hardly even talked to him." His voice
cracked.

"Dad! Uncle Matt — he's Midnight Smith! He can
handle anything! Even the valley — he's talked about
it, been there. He's got survival gear."

"He's gone down in the valley," Dad said, as if in a
trance.

"He'll radio in. He'll — " But I felt sick. I couldn't
stand to even think about it. "Dad, we've got to find
him!"

"We can't — not unless we hire an airplane, and
there's none available. All are working round the clock,
hauling cargo and equipment to finish the road. And I
can't leave the mill, your mom, Jody."

"You can't. But I can."

Dad looked at me, and his face showed the first sign
of hope since he'd read the notice.

"You can't walk there. I don't know how . . ."

"I'll figure a way, real soon." I hesitated, my mind
racing. Then I looked at Dad. "We're expecting a supply
plane, aren't we?"

"Yes."

Our eyes met, and a look of understanding passed
between us.

We went back to the mill and told Mom the awful
news. At first she refused to even think about me going
to search for my uncle. Then, as Dad said nothing, Mom

sighed and said something about "leaving it to chance."
She knew none of us would rest until he'd been found.

"Chance" came sooner than later.

The next morning, we heard a plane overhead. Mom,
Jody, and I ran down to the river. Jody pointed to the
airplane, saying, "Uncle Matt! Uncle Matt!"

But as it taxied in, I could see it wasn't a yellow
Norseman, and the pilot was a stranger. We pulled him
in.

"You're Jedediah Smith?" the pilot shouted from
above. I shook my head and pointed to Dad, hanging
back.

The pilot removed his goggles and jumped to shore.
He went to Dad and stuck out his hand. "I'm Benjamin
Walker. The police asked me to stop in."

Dad shook his hand. "Come on back to the shack."

Mr. Walker hesitated. "I got some news. Not too good,
I'm afraid."

I couldn't stand seeing the pain in Dad's eyes.

"A trapper reported your brother's crashed plane to
the trader at Bare Bones Landing. There was no sign of
life."

"You're sure?" Dad said.

The pilot nodded.

"Isn't anyone going in?"

"We took Chimo — the trapper — and flew over. But
we couldn't land. It's wartime, you know. Here and
overseas, every available pilot is being worked to death.
We're losing a couple of our boys every month."

Mom started to cry. Dad reached over and gathered
her in his arms.

"I'm sorry," Mr. Walker said. "I'm delivering another
load up to Bare Bones. I'll make sure they've done all
they can."

Dad's eyes were shut tight. "Oh God, I'm sorry," he
whispered into Mom's hair.

"He knew that you loved him," Mom said.

I ran into the woods then, crashing through the trees toward the river, not caring where I was going. My Uncle Matthew couldn't be dead! Finally I collapsed against a balm tree, pounding at its trunk until my fists were raw and the bark stained with blood.

Conda nudged my hand, and I hugged her to me. "Oh, Conda," I sobbed. Together we watched the mist rise off the Liard River.

18

Stowaways

BLAST JAPS FROM ATTU AND AGATTU AS
ENEMY MAKES STAND ON KISKA

Blasted by American sea and air power, the
Japanese appear to have fled today from two of
three Aleutian Islands they occupied four
months ago and were undergoing heavy
bombardment on their remaining foothold.

"We're going to find him, Conda."

I went back to camp and into the cookshack where
Mom and Dad were talking with the pilot.

"Dad?" I said, "Can I go?"

"What? Oh, yeah." He coughed. "Benjamin, could you
take my son out with you to the landing there? He wants
to go in to the valley."

"What for? I told you nothing could have survived that
crash. It's crazy. Snow's coming, and it's deep wilderness, boy."

"I'm not scared of the wilderness, and I want to go."

"Well, you'll have to find someone else to take you. I
won't and I can't. I'm on U.S. Army contract, can't

transport civilians without special permission. Takes days for an application to go through, and you have to have a good reason."

"I guess you'll have to wait, son," Dad said. His eyes met mine.

I waited until the conversation had resumed, then quietly slipped out the door.

Conda and I went over to the skid shack. I stuffed an extra pair of socks in my bedroll, grabbed my rifle and a pocketful of ammunition, and the Player's flat-fifty tin I'd been using for a bank. What else? Mom had brought out a plate of cookies for us to snack on before bedtime. I filled my other pocket. I looked for a piece of paper to scribble out a note, and found the map Uncle Matthew had drawn of the valley on the back of a fuel bill. I stuffed it into my pocket, too. I ripped a page out of my school notebook, wrote a note to Mom and Dad, and stuck it on Dad's pillow.

When we'd made sure the coast was clear, I skirted around the cookshack and down to the plane tied to the dock. Conda whined and ran in circles in front of me.

"You can't come, girl." She looked up at me, pranced in a circle, and headed onto the dock. "Okay, you win. But you'll have to keep quiet."

I opened the plane's cargo door, lifted Conda inside, threw in my bedroll, and climbed aboard. It was a big plane, a single-engine Ford, and Walker had quite a load on: bags of vegetables, cases of canned goods, mail, kegs of nails, a case of whiskey, all kinds of junk. I crouched behind a bag of onions, pulled Conda near me, wrapped a piece of rope around her neck, and clamped my hand around her muzzle. "Sorry, girl."

Footsteps were getting closer. "Hush, Conda." The pilot got in, muttered to himself as he checked the controls, and started the engine. The plane bumped along the river in preparation for takeoff.

I held Conda tightly so she wouldn't roll around or bark. What she did, I couldn't prevent. She got sick. I held her head away from my feet, then surveyed the mess. The roar of the engine blotted out any noise — but the smell! I grabbed a sack of onions and lowered it overtop the vomit. The combination of odours was enough to gag a maggot, but I hoped Mr. Walker would think it was just some rotten produce. Conda looked so miserable that I might have laughed if we hadn't been fugitives on an important mission.

A couple of hours later we landed. The pilot got out, and I could hear someone tie up the plane.

"Want to unload now?"

"Naw, I'm too tired. Let's go have a drink first."

When they were gone, Conda and I cautiously sneaked out.

We'd landed on a lake in front of a little trading post. A few Indian tents surrounded the post. Moose hides dried on racks in the clearing, and two skinny dogs ran toward us barking. The hair on Conda's back stood in a ridge, and the dogs backed off.

I took Uncle Matt's map out of my pocket and decided we must have landed on Tea Boily Lake.

I walked over to an Indian man. "I'm looking for a guy named Chimo," I said. The man answered in his native language and pointed toward the post. I had no choice but to go inside.

Around the pot-bellied stove sat three men, one dressed in a shirt and pants, who I thought must be the trading post manager, and a man in a moose-hide jacket, likely the trapper, and the pilot.

"Thanks for the ride, Mr. Walker," I said.

"I *thought* I was a bit heavy in the tail! What are you doing here, boy?"

MIDNIGHT SMITH'S MAP OF
THE VALLEY OF LOST PLANES

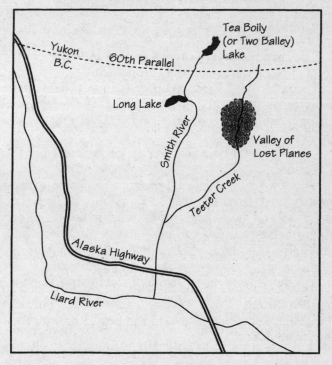

"I'm going to find my uncle."

"You're crazy! Chimo here found the broken prop." The pilot nodded toward the trapper.

"That the Norseman that disappeared from the rescue mission?" the trader asked.

"That's the one," the pilot said.

The trapper stopped picking his teeth. "He's gone."

"How do I get in there?"

The trader looked at me like I was crazy. "Hills getting snow," he said.

"I'll find it."

The men laughed. I turned around to leave.

"I'm going that way," the trapper said.

Benjamin Walker stood up. "Better yet, help me unload the plane, and I'll take you home. You could get me in big trouble with the U.S. Army with your foolishness, you know!"

"I'm sorry. I'll help you, to pay for my ride, but then I'm gone."

When we were finished, I bought a few basic supplies, mostly food, from the trader. Benjamin Walker shook my hand and gave Conda a pat. "Just make sure I don't have to give your dad bad news about you, too, son."

I helped Chimo load his supplies onto his pack dogs and Conda, then our own packs on packboards.

We headed southeast through the bush. Chimo told me his mother was Athapaskan Indian and his father a French-Canadian trader.

"I've been trapping the Yukon-B.C. border area since I was a pup," he said. He looked pretty old now, but he sure was in good shape. His moose-hide jacket was every colour except the original one, and he wore heavy black pants. His dark hair was thick and long, and it looked like he'd cut it with a knife. Chimo turned his gaunt, whiskerless face and peered at me intently with jet black eyes that seemed to look right through me.

"The valley's haunted," he said. "Prospectors used to go there for gold, but not now. Saw strange lights. Heard sounds that froze their blood." He leaned toward me, until I could feel his breath. His voice lowered. "I saw spirits! Never stay there now."

I waited for him to go on, to explain, if there was an explanation.

He started walking faster, until I had to dogtrot to keep up.

"I was trapping. Bad night. Wind blowing, fire going out. I try to sleep. I close my eyes. Coals start to flame! Other side of the fire, a man squats down. A pilot. Pokes coals with a stick. He looks at me, stands up, backs away. I hold my gun all night. Saw him no more."

"That's weird!" I was panting hard now. "Maybe he lived near there."

"Nobody lives there."

"No Indians or anyone?"

"Scared. Too many spirits." He stopped suddenly. "It's not just Valley of Lost Planes. It's Valley of Lost Souls."

We talked no more, saving our energy for the hike. When we came to the top of a hill, Chimo pointed to an old game trail that followed a creek, which Uncle Matt's map said was Teeter Creek. We shifted Conda's load onto his dogs, then I thanked him and started walking. It would take me today and the better part of the next day to reach the pass.

I shot a rabbit and cooked it that night over a campfire. Conda and I ate the rabbit and some cookies, then curled up and went to sleep.

That night I had a dream. An old flier wearing a scarred leather jacket, a white silk scarf around his neck, leather helmet, and goggles was trying to tell me something, but I couldn't hear over the roar of planes. I woke up as dawn was breaking over the ridge of hills.

It was snowing lightly, and there was an inch or so on the ground but not enough to hide the Norseman's yellow fuselage. Actually, the snow gave me hope: I'd be able to track animals better. And if Uncle Matthew was alive, I'd see his signs — footprints, blazes on trees, messages scratched on rocks.

By the time I got through the pass, the snow had stopped and a pale sun shone over the distant mountains. Looking down toward the valley, still shrouded in purple shadow, I could make out a creek snaking through the bottom. The world below was perfectly still — no sounds, no campfire smoke, no movement except for a couple of hawks circling slowly over the treetops.

I started down the trail, praying it would lead me to my Uncle Matthew.

19

Valley of Lost Planes

CANADIANS AND AMERICANS FLY WING TO
WING GUARDING ALASKA'S SHORES

I hiked all day on a trail that looked like it hadn't been travelled by anything but wild animals, and made camp as the sun dropped behind the ridge. I hadn't seen any game, so Conda and I ate the last of the rabbit and some bannock I made, topped off with a half-dozen cookies. Conda seemed restless, running into the bush then back again to sit by the fire and whine. She was spooking me, and I regretted bringing her.

I fell asleep by the fire, but awoke an hour or so later with the feeling something was watching me. The night sounds seemed ordinary: a wolf howled down in the draw, some coyotes were trying to imitate him, and occasionally an owl twittered. Then came a whispering sound.

But there was no wind.

It came again, a blend of voices, all static as if coming over radios.

"Operation Wolverine, ready stage one."

"Foreign object sited. Valley pass. Hold. Stop."

"Re-locate foreign object."

"Stage two."

Conda's ears lay flat on her head as she slunk closer to the fire, almost stepping on me. I sat up in my sleeping bag, holding my rifle.

A series of lights came out of the west, slowly mounting in the sky. They got brighter as they flew near, passed overhead, fixing me in spotlights, then swooped past to disappear on the far side of the valley. I heard another sound, like the whoosh of air blowing through a wind tunnel. I smudged my fire and lay low.

The sky lightened as the moon rose over the ridge. A fighter plane roared over my head. Then another, and another. Four planes, engines thundering! Staccato shots rang out as rounds of ammunition were fired into the valley.

Nobody had better fool with me! I pulled my rifle closer, my finger shaking on the trigger, and checked to make sure my hunting knife was in its sheath.

Then their lights, red and green, on, off, arced over the mountain ridge away from the Valley of Lost Planes.

I finally slept as dawn broke.

It was full daylight when I awoke, and I was freezing. There was no point in lighting the fire; I ate some cold bannock and a couple more cookies. Conda and I started off again. About two hundred feet from the campfire I saw the tracks of two huge timber wolves that had sat and watched us last night.

Chimo had told me that Uncle Matthew's plane went down seven miles from the other side of the pass. Around noon I found a small path that led off the trail and through some pines. I followed it until the path seemed to end at a keystone arch built into a side hill. Then behind some bushes I saw a door made of rawhide stretched over a frame. There was no junk outside, no pelts or mining tools, no wash basin or snowshoes or any other stuff. Just a propeller hanging above the portal of what I realized was an old abandoned mine.

I called, "Hello, the house!" the usual greeting when coming upon an isolated cabin. A weird voice answered. I couldn't make out what it said, so I repeated, "Hello, the house!" Again I heard a strange response. I pulled aside the door and went inside.

The entrance was a four-foot-high tunnel. Hunching over, I made my way down it into a room whose only light was from a small hole in the roof. I straightened up and looked around. On the walls, which were shored up by logs, were pictures of pinup girls. I recognized Betty Grable because Uncle Matthew had her picture in his plane. There were old grenades, ribbons, and medals, Victory Bond posters, props from planes. An American army coat hung from a nail. Army pistols and brass-plated rifles were mounted above the doors.

"Hello!" I called, and nearly jumped out of my skin when a voice behind me croaked, "C-B-J! Cleared to land! Cleared to land!" I whirled around. Perched over the doorway sat a huge raven. Conda went crazy, barking, then running in circles. "Shut up!" said the bird. Conda did, and hid under the table. The raven and I stared at each other. It cried again, "May Day! May Day! No joy! No joy!" I heard a boom from deep inside the cave.

Conda and I hightailed it outside. "Let's wait here, girl," I said, patting her head to calm us both. "We don't want to surprise whoever lives there, do we?" Conda seemed to agree, and we perched on some fallen logs near the mine's entrance, where we had a good view of the door and path.

A man appeared in the doorway. He had wild tufts of

hair on each side of his shiny bald head. His pale
eyes shifted from me to Conda, to the sky, to the
ground, left, right, up, down. A little tongue gathered
up some snuff juice that had seeped out the sides of
his mouth.

"They're not yours," he said, eyeing me like I was
stealing the logs on which I sat. "They're mine." He
spoke with an accent that I thought might be British.

"What's yours?"

"The airplanes. The bombers. I found them, and
they're mine."

Conda started wagging her tail. I couldn't believe it.
Here we were, hundreds of miles from help, and Conda
had taken a liking to a raving lunatic!

"I don't want your bombers," I said, hoping my heart
would slow to normal and I'd stop stuttering.

"Then you may enter." He stood aside to let me into
the tunnel. I had no choice since my faithful dog had
already brushed past him and gone inside.

"I'm Jay Smith," I said. "Chimo brought me to the
forks."

"I seen 'im."

"Who're you?"

"Lieutenant John Elias Johnson. You can call me
Goldbug. And this is my girlfriend, Rebecca," he said,
indicating the raven.

"Do you know my Uncle Matthew? Midnight Smith?
He went missing — " I couldn't finish.

"What does he fly?" Goldbug asked.

"A yellow Norseman. He was looking for the bombers."

"Ah yes. I saw it. But that one's not mine yet. Not until
he leaves."

"The pilot? Is my uncle alive?"

But Goldbug stopped talking. A cunning look crossed

his face. He grinned, exposing black gums and worn brown stumps of teeth.

"They mostly all leave when they land in the valley. But not me. I won't leave my ship. Neither will he — your uncle."

"But . . . nobody knows about you! How do you live?"

He smiled, his eyes looking from one wall of his cave to the other. "Lots of supplies. Planes are loaded with rations. I've got enough canned bully beef to see me through a *third* world war! They leave me their food, they leave me their clothes, and they leave me their airplanes."

"Then you're the ghost Chimo saw — "

"I'm not a ghost, lad! As I live and breathe, I'm more real than any of 'em. Pinch me." He held out a skinny arm. I pinched it. The flesh was warm.

"Aye, I've got enough supplies laid in here to live like a king. You hungry, lad?"

"Yes."

He turned and went over to the stove, poked around in the coals until he'd brought the fire up, and put on the kettle. He took a cast-iron skillet from a hook, threw in some grease and laid some kind of meat in the pan. Then he began to whip up a batch of bannock. The smell of food brought me down to earth.

As dinner cooked, Goldbug started fiddling with a two-way plane radio. A signal came in clearly, announcing the latest news.

"Three cargo trucks reached Whitehorse on October 1, carrying loads all the way from Dawson Creek. The pilot run took six days, and they're now on their way back. They should reach Dawson Creek on the sixth if everything goes well. The tote road is now complete!

"The highway to Alaska, life tendon to America's Achilles' heel, is scheduled to be opened about December 1, months ahead of schedule, according to Secretary of War, Henry L. Stimson. Military supplies, heretofore airborne, will be rushed by truck to remote aerial and military bases until April and May, when thaws will further challenge the ingenuity of army engineers."

He twirled the switch.

"This is in truth a people's war. It is a war that cannot be regarded as won until the fundamental rights of the people of the earth are secured. So declared Sumner Welles, Undersecretary of State . . ."

Goldbug grinned. "I'm as up-to-date as someone in New York City."

He did a little jig over to the stove.

"Down went the gunner, and then the gunner's mate," he sang. "Up jumped the Sky Pilot and gave the boys a look, and manned the gun himself as he laid aside the Book. Shouting 'Praise the Lord, and pass the ammunition!'" He swung the wooden spoon in a circle above his head. Rebecca cackled and Conda barked madly.

Suddenly he turned to look at me.

"You want a bath?"

"A what?"

"A bath! Get that soot off you. Here." He indicated for me to follow him down the tunnel. Rounding a curve, he led me into a little cave branching out from the main mine shaft. He lit a bitch light, made from a rag dipped in a dish of coyote grease, and set it on the ground. In the centre of the cave was a small steaming pool.

"Natural hot spring. Keeps the place warm and me from getting too lousy!" He flashed me a black grin. "Jump in, lad. I'll have tea ready by the time you're done."

Shivering, I tossed my clothes into a corner of the cave. Conda sat down to wait as I lowered myself into the pool, sinking until just my nose and eyes were above the steaming hot water. Hard limestone rock formed the sides and bottom of the sulphur pool, which smelled of rotten eggs. I moved from the edge, trying to test the depth. My feet couldn't touch bottom. I looked up and watched the lamp light flickering on the dripping stalactites overhead.

I could hear Goldbug carrying on a conversation with the raven. After a few minutes I got out, dried off with my shirt, and went back to the first room.

"Where did you get all this stuff?" I asked. I pointed around the cave.

"Oh, some I brought from the front," he said. "I was a Lieutenant in the Great War. Flew a biplane for Britain's Royal Aero Club." He indicated an old leather helmet, goggles, and a yellowed flying scarf displayed on a shelf. "Pilots really had to know what they were doing, then."

"Your accent — it's English?"

"I'm a Lancashire lad. I fought England's war, and when it was over I got as far away as possible from bloody so-called civilization. And I'm going to stay right here and see the sun come up over these mountains as long as I live."

"You were a pilot?"

"Still am! Since 1913 in the Great War. Got me a bag of medals somewhere. Aren't worth nothing. War heroes are a dime a dozen. The live ones, that is. Dead ones live on. People talk about their victories forever. You play crib?"

"Yeah, but my uncle!"

"He's not moving. C'mon. One game before I feed you. Then I'll take you to the crash site. Ah, the world's going so fast nowadays. Live heros have to keep on competing or they're nothing. Me, I'm lucky. I'm still flying."

He dealt the cards. The crib board was a moose horn, the pegs were bone.

"You have a plane?" I asked.

"Dozens of 'em. Bombers! Gliders! Fighter planes! Buzzbomb bush planes — little mosquitos like that yellow fella!"

The raven came down and sat on the edge of the table, picking at our pegs, changing the score. Goldbug laughed. "You're my copilot, aren't you, Rebecca? She flies with me everywhere."

"She helps you win, too," I said, as Rebecca gave Goldbug another twenty points.

I went over to the wall to look at a propeller. I touched its cold metal, running my fingers over the broken shaft, and a shiver went through me.

"Come on, sit up to the table, now."

His food was delicious, and I made a pig of myself by asking for seconds. Goldbug chuckled, and loaded my plate.

When we'd finished eating, I again tried to get Goldbug to take me to the crash site. "My uncle — " I began, but he interrupted impatiently.

"He's there, sonny. I saw him go down. He'll be a hero now. Don't worry, you can see him soon. He's not goin' anywhere. You don't fly without one of those things."

"What happened?"

"A spot of bad luck. Lost his prop."

"He couldn't land anyway?"

"Nope. Prop goes, part flies off, airplane shakes like the dickens, feels like the engine's gonna fly right out of it. He throttles the engine back — he's coming to the valley, looks good. Tries to glide downhill, thinks he can make it. Too low, trees are there, snag comes through — and gets him. Another deadly mistake."

I didn't want to hear the rest, but Goldbug went on.

"Should have turned around when he had height, and landed going uphill in the tops of the trees. But, it can happen to anybody. No matter how good you are. It can happen — and I'll quote those words to my dyin' day."

"I can't believe he's gone!"

"He isn't gone, son. He's there. The folks in the bombers, now, they've all gone. I showed 'em a way out. Ten on each plane, and they all walked out. But they left their airplanes for me."

"Last night I heard sounds," I said. "Like fighter planes or something, and hundreds of shots."

"Ah, yes, they're trying to destroy my bombers, make sure they're out of commission. They sneak in at night and strafe 'em until they're ripped full of holes. If the enemy finds them, they won't be able to fly them out, get their technical secrets."

"But they could kill someone! My uncle's there!"

"No, not near the bombers. He's about five miles further on." He chucked the raven's feathers with his finger. "They'll leave 'em alone now. They go over once, is all."

"Who?"

The cunning look came over his face again. "I know who they are. I pick up their frequency. I hear 'em. But they don't know about me, or they'd come after me. I know things."

"Oh."

"And I'm smart enough to keep my mouth shut. Then the bombers are mine forever."

I lay back on some caribou hides, Conda at my side. Just for a moment, I thought, and then I'll make Goldbug take me there. The propeller shone softly in the flickering light from the wood fire. I was dog-tired, but I wasn't going to fall asleep. Uncle Matthew had walked out of crashes before. Maybe he carried an extra prop, or was carving one out of wood. We'd leave the valley together.

The next thing I knew, Rebecca was squawking, "Get up, lazy bones!"

20

A Tip of the Wings

ALASKA HIGHWAY OPEN TO TRAFFIC

Trucks Moving Supplies to Northern Pacific
Outposts.

"Now I'll show you my private air force," Goldbug announced, when he saw I was awake. "Real beauties. You can even pilot one."

He was a strange man, all right, but only he knew where my uncle was. I had to get him to take me there.

"Do you fly every day?" I asked.

"Every day."

"How do you get in and out of the valley when no one else seems to make it?"

"I'm the world's best!"

He tucked some bannock in a sack, along with some tea leaves in a little jar. Then he lead me down a goat path through a mist of ice crystals that hadn't decided if they were snow or fog toward the basin of the valley.

We stood on a precipice and looked down. "The Valley of Lost Planes," I said. Although my voice was barely above a whisper, it carried on an echo.

"They can call my place what they want — Uncle Sam's Million Dollar Valley, Valley of Lost Planes, Valley of Lost Bombers. But they're *not* lost. They're all right here. Six of them this year."

"What if someone comes to take them out?"

"Never will. Cost a fortune to airlift them. Not worth it. I'm the only pilot who could do it. So they wreck them. When this war is over, nobody will give a tinker's toot about them anyway. Folks will be more concerned about building factories and getting rich again."

We hiked for miles. I could hardly keep up with Goldbug. Although he was old, he had a mile-eating stride that left me panting behind him. We reached a point on the goat trail where I was afraid if I looked past my feet I'd fall down the sharp cliff.

"Look over there." Goldbug pointed a mile or so down the valley. "Tell me what you see."

I braced myself against the cliff wall and looked down. Trees and rocks. "Nothing."

"Look again," he commanded.

I did as he said but could see nothing.

"My beauties," he said. "Reclining on that little plateau."

I looked hard where he'd indicated, and saw the sun glint off a piece of metal. Then I saw them: three giant planes, camouflage-coloured, nestling on a small flat piece of open land. Goldbug's beauties were the lost Marauders.

He scurried down the path, shale and pebbles tumbling from his footsteps. I followed cautiously, picking my way among the loose rocks.

"Look — these last three are in perfect shape!" he said. "The pilots got low on fuel. Talked it over on their intercoms and decided to crash land.

"They couldn't have picked a better spot: a mile square, no trees, just patches of Arctic bush. They left their gear up and landed one by one, a hundred feet apart. Perfect job! And in perfect weather! Ripped the bellies of the planes some, but nobody got hurt. And they left me their babies for showing them the way out."

Goldbug ran up to the first bomber and climbed inside. I stared up at the toothless old flier sitting proudly in the cockpit of the B-26. He indicated for me to climb up and gestured to the copilot's seat. The plane was in pretty good shape, if you overlooked the ripped underside, a shredded wing or two, and, of course, the ceiling vented with bullet holes from the strafing operation.

"Fly like a pro, boy!" Goldbug's voice seemed to change as he barked out commands. "Check list! Throttles: closed. Mixture: full rich. Petrol: on. Mags: on, both. Standby to start number one!"

Feeling like a fool, I said, "Check."

"Start engine! Good. Stand by number two."

"Roger."

"Start engine." He whistled shrilly imitating the whine of a starter. Suddenly there was silence.

"What's wrong?" I asked.

Goldbug's face folded into a grin. "We're out of petrol."

We sat staring ahead through the broken windscreen.

"Where are the other pilots?" I asked. "They were still missing when I left."

"I walked 'em through to a back pass. They'll get back to civilization in a week or so. They had enough rations to keep 'em happy." He started shutting down the airplane as if it were really running. "Mixture: full lean. Throttle: closed. Switches: off. Petrol: off. Radios: off." He turned to me. "The other bombers are in pretty good shape, too, but this is my favourite. You can use one of my Martins, but you've got to leave it hangared here when you're done flying."

"I need to find my uncle," I said. "Maybe he's hurt."

"Nay, he's not hurting," Goldbug said. "I'll show you

where he landed. You can make it yourself. It's not more than five miles."

We got out of the bomber. Goldbug pointed over the valley. I could see bits of wreckage strewn over the hillsides, blue and yellow and orange pieces of metal and canvas that had once belonged to the fuselages of a dozen planes.

"Those fellows didn't know anything about flying in northern conditions," Goldbug said. "American pilots, used to fancy airports and radios that work. Poor devils didn't have a chance — got tossed around like feathers in the wind. Lost their bearings. Mostly all new pilots."

"My uncle's American, but he's a northern flier." I didn't look at Goldbug but stared down at the valley floor. "I went looking for him soon as I saw him go down. He's still at the controls. It's still his plane."

Goldbug pointed to where I'd find the Norseman. I thanked him and left. He was back in his bomber before Conda and I had reached the first bend in the trail.

The sun came out and glinted off bits of metal strewn throughout the bush. I picked up a piece with part of a serial number on it. Then I tossed it and its story back into the bushes, not wanting to think what had caused it to come to rest there.

The sun disappeared behind a cloud, and a cold wind whipped up skiffs of snow. The sky darkened. "We might get a storm, Conda," I said as we trudged on down the path. A sound. I stopped, listening intently. An airplane was roaring up the valley. I looked up, expecting to see the plane's wings passing overhead, but there was nothing at all, just the sound of an engine. I followed the course the phantom plane seemed to be taking. "Come on, Conda," I said. "It's trying to tell us something."

The roar returned. As it passed overhead, I held my hands over my ears to muffle the deafening engine noise, then ran after the sound, which faded as suddenly as a memory, and I could no longer be sure if it was real or imagined. I trudged on another half mile, following the direction of the phantom plane. Suddenly there it was, a yellow blotch on the hillside.

I ran toward the crash site, my beating heart the only sound. Ahead, a broken yellow wing stuck up from the buck brush. And then I saw the call letters on the wing: NC-195N.

The rest of the plane lay a couple hundred feet away. I crept toward it. Conda slunk behind me, ears back, tail down.

Nellie's fuselage was ripped to shreds, flipped over on its back with the tail fin and rudder twisted. The tail itself had been sheared off. One wing, the wing I'd spotted, had been torn away, the other was still attached but mangled and twisted. The cowling had collapsed, and the propless engine had been pushed back into the cockpit by the force of the crash. The windshield had exploded, and snags and branches were sticking into the cabin.

I couldn't see inside.

I was afraid to open the pilot's door. "Please, God, someone, help me . . ."

I tugged at the cargo door.

The cold still air inside the plane almost choked me. It smelled as Nellie always smelled — of gasoline and fish.

I looked toward the cockpit. A hunk of black wolf fur quivered in the twisted frame of the windshield. But Midnight Smith was no longer at the controls.

I crawled along the ceiling, over junk scattered helter-skelter throughout the plane and freed the fur, turning it over in my hand to see if it would give me any clues. A little patch of fabric on the back showed that it had been ripped from Uncle Matt's parka.

Conda whined from down below. "Don't cry, Conda,

don't cry," I said, wiping my cheeks with the backs of my hands. The plane shuddered in the wind, and a blast of fine snow smacked against it. I could find no note, no sign of blood, nothing to indicate what might have happened.

I crawled to the back of the plane, looking, through an annoying blur of tears, for some sign that would give me a message. Snowshoes. Cross-cut saw. Some traps and a first-aid kit. Uncle Matthew's leather briefcase. I opened it up. There were letters inside, the aircraft repair log, maps, an airman's watch with a broken strap, and some documents. But no pilot's log book!

I started throwing stuff around. Where was his rifle? And shells? Axe? Ration kit? I desperately hoped I wouldn't find what I was looking for.

The sounds of my panting breath echoed in the plane as I madly sorted through the wreckage. Finally I sat back, exhausted. I'd found nothing. I stood, and felt something hit my head. I looked up.

Then I started to laugh. Conda looked up, too, turning her head to one side as she tried to understand my crazy behaviour. A piece of cardboard anchored in the upside-down seat had flipped my hair as I passed underneath it. I tugged it out. A note was scribbled on it.

I'm hurt. Going to follow the creek, try to find the Alaska Highway.

Midnight Smith.

"The creek!" I yelled. Conda began wagging her tail. I threw Uncle Matt's briefcase, his flare gun and flares out through the open door. Then I shoved the piece of fur into my pocket and climbed out of the plane.

"Goldbug said he walked the other pilots out the back pass, Conda! Uncle Matt must have been in a coma when Goldbug found him — if he found him at all — and when he came to he went out the other way!"

I shut the door behind me, still babbling to the dog, and gave Nellie a farewell slap.

"The Wolf Man's gonna make it, Conda! He's got ammunition and an axe and food. He knows these rivers and valleys — he and Nellie have seen them all! He'll blaze a trail out to the Alaska Highway!"

Conda and I hiked until the snow-shrouded sun dropped behind the ridge and it got too dark to see any signs that might have been left on the scrubby trees. As dusk fell the snow stopped and moonlight silvered the trail. I listened for foreign sounds — engines, shots, radio calls, but there was only silence, broken occasionally by a gust of wind. Goldbug said the fighter planes wouldn't likely be back again, but I was scared he might be wrong — for the second time.

When we came to an overhanging rock, I made a lean-to "siwash" camp at its base, where I felt protected. I thought it must be around ten o'clock, but it was hard to tell. Northern Lights streaked the sky pale green, slithering the width of the valley.

A wolf howled, then another, until we were surrounded by a northern opera and I couldn't tell what were howls and what were echoes. Conda sat, ears perked, looking over the valley. Then she got up and paced back and forth in front of the cliff, as if responding to sounds too sensitive for human ears. I fell asleep, letting her and the wolves watch over me.

My dream was of an old World War One pilot in full flying gear — leather helmet, goggles, white silk scarf — walking away from a downed biplane. Before disappearing, he turned and gave me a thumbs-up signal. It was Lieutenant John Elias "Goldbug" Johnson.

The next morning as we passed on the ridge above Goldbug's cave, I waved and hollered "Halloo!" but received no response. I hoped that he would never be chased out of his valley — let him live with his flying ghosts!

Around noon I reached the top of the pass. Just as I was about to descend the winding game trail, I heard the drone of an airplane. It was probably another phantom, so I didn't even look up as the noise passed overhead. Then I saw a real plane heading toward the horizon. I fired one of Uncle Matt's red flares. The plane kept going for endless seconds, then circled back and flew right at me, rocking its wings.

As it got nearer I could see it was Benjamin Walker's Ford! Almost overhead now it dipped low, and I could see someone was with him — someone who looked a lot like my dad and me. I waved my arms wildly, and the man waved back, then threw out a package. I ran to retrieve it. The pilot rocked his wings and went on ahead as I picked up the burlap sack.

Inside was a loaf of bread, a hunk of cheese, and a note.

Follow the creek to the highway. Will meet you.

Midnight.

I broke into a run to keep up with Conda, along the Wolf Man's trail from the Valley of Lost Planes to the Alaska Highway.

Epilogue

On October 25, 1942, crews made contact twenty miles south of the Yukon-Alaska border at Beaver Creek (Mile 1,202) to close the northern sector of the Alcan highway project. Two Caterpillar tractors plunged through the bush from opposite directions, one from the north operated by the white 18th Regiment of Engineers and one from the south operated by the black 97th Regiment, and touched noses. The job was done.

An official opening ceremony was held at Soldiers Summit on Kluane lake on November 20, 1942. Mom, Dad, Jody, and I flew up for the celebration with Uncle Matt in his new airplane, a four-seater yellow Waco.

U.S. War Secretary Stimson congratulated the ten thousand soldiers, from seven army engineer regiments, and six thousand civilian workers, who had built the pioneer road in eight months and twelve days, at the rate of eight miles a day. I felt kind of proud that we'd helped provide the timber for some of the bridges that were needed to cross two hundred rivers.

Even though the highway was supposed to be top secret, the first public announcement of the completion of the Alcan, now called the Alaska Highway, came over Japanese radio.

People in the North say that a man died for every mile built on the Alaska Highway: 1,523 miles, 1,523 men.

Perhaps it's true.